ROCHDALE
BOROUGH COUNCIL

Please return/renew this item by the last date shown. Books may also be renewed by phone: 0 300 303 8876 or on web: www.roc h s es

Chantelle Shaw lives on the Kent coast, five minutes from the sea, and does much of her thinking about the characters in her books while walking on the beach. She's been an avid reader from an early age. Her schoolfriends used to hide their books when she visited—but Chantelle would retreat into her own world, and still writes stories in her head all the time. Chantelle has been blissfully married to her own tall, dark and very patient hero for over twenty years, and has six children. She began to read Mills & Boon® as a teenager, and throughout the years of being a stay-at-home mum to her brood found romantic fiction helped her to stay sane! She enjoys reading and writing about strong-willed, feisty women, and even stronger-willed sexy heroes. Chantelle is at her happiest when writing. She is particularly inspired while cooking dinner, which unfortunately results in a lot of culinary disasters! She also loves gardening, walking, and eating chocolate (followed by more walking!). Catch up with Chantelle's latest news on her website: www.chantelleshaw.com

Recent titles by the same author:

A DANGEROUS INFATUATION
AFTER THE GREEK AFFAIR
THE ULTIMATE RISK

BEHIND THE CASTELLO DOORS

BY
CHANTELLE SHAW

First published in Great Britain 2012
by Mills & Boon, an imprint of Harlequin (UK) Limited.
Harlequin (UK) Limited, Eton House, 18-24 Paradise Road,
Richmond, Surrey TW9 1SR

© Chantelle Shaw 2012

ISBN: 978 0 263 89073 0

Harlequin (UK) policy is to use papers that are natural, renewable and recyclable products and made from wood grown in sustainable forests. The logging and manufacturing process conform to the legal environmental regulations of the country of origin.

Printed and bound in Spain
by Blackprint CPI, Barcelona

BEHIND THE
CASTELLO DOORS

For
Patrick, Adam,
Rosie, Lucy,
William and Oliver.
My six wonderful children who are now amazing adults.
You make me happy (and turn my hair grey)!

CHAPTER ONE

THE road twisted up the mountainside like a sinuous black snake, its wet surface gleaming in the glow from the car headlamps. The rain seemed to fall harder the higher they climbed. They had left Oliena some fifteen minutes ago, and as the car rounded another bend Beth watched the lights from the town disappear from view.

She leaned forward in her seat to speak to the taxi driver. 'How much farther?'

She had already discovered that he spoke little English and sighed when he shrugged. But perhaps he had understood her, because a few moments later he glanced over his shoulder.

'Soon you see Castello del Falco…er…Castle of the Falcon, I think is how you say,' he explained in a heavy accent.

Beth frowned. 'You mean Mr Piras actually lives in a real castle?' She had assumed that the owner of the Piras-Cossu Bank's private residence in Sardinia would be a luxurious villa, and that 'castle' was simply an extravagant title he had given to his home.

The taxi driver did not reply, but as the car crested another ridge of the Gennargentu Mountains, Beth caught her breath at the sight of a great grey fortress looming out of the darkness. Peering through the rain, she saw that the road stretched ahead until it disappeared through a cavernous black gateway. The outer walls of the castle were illuminated by lamps which revealed the sheer vastness of the structure, and grotesque gargoyles leered out of the shadows like portents of doom.

For heaven's sake! She gave herself a mental shake, angry that she had allowed her imagination to run away with her. But as the taxi drew nearer to the castle entrance she could not dismiss an inexplicable feeling of apprehension, and she was tempted to ask the driver to turn around and take her back to the town. Maybe she was being over-imaginative, but she sensed that her life would change for ever if she crossed the threshold of the Castello del Falco.

She had come to Sardinia for Sophie's sake, she reminded herself, glancing at the baby-carrier affixed to the seat beside her. She could not turn back now. Nevertheless, her heart lurched as the car sped between the black gates, and she cast a last look behind her, feeling as though she had passed from a safe and familiar world into the unknown.

The party was in full swing. From his vantage point on the balcony overlooking the ballroom Cesario Piras watched the guests dancing and drinking champagne, and through a doorway leading to the banqueting hall he could see more people crowded around tables laden with food.

He was glad they were enjoying themselves. His staff worked hard, and deserved his thanks with this lavish reception in recognition of their services to the Piras-Cossu Bank. The guests were not to know that their host was counting the hours until he could be alone again. He regretted now that he had not instructed his PA to rearrange the date she had picked for the party. Donata had only worked for him for a few months, and was unaware that the third of March was a date that would forever be branded on Cesario's soul.

Unconsciously he traced his fingers over the deep scar that began at the corner of his left eye and sliced down his cheek to his mouth. Today was the fourth anniversary of his son's death. Time had moved on inexorably, and the savage grief he'd felt in the first months and years after the tragedy had slowly turned to dull acceptance. But anniversaries were always difficult. He had sanctioned the party date hoping that his duties as host would distract his thoughts. But all evening images of Nicolo had filled his mind, and the memories had evoked a pain inside him that felt like a knife through his heart.

A faint noise from behind him alerted Cesario to the fact that he was no longer alone. He swung round, his frown clearing when he saw his butler.

'What is it, Teodoro?'

'A young woman has arrived at the castle and has asked to see you, *signor*.'

Cesario glanced at his watch. 'A guest has arrived this late?'

'She is not a party guest. But she is most insistent that she must speak with you.' Teodoro could not hide his disapproval as he recalled the bedraggled-looking woman shrouded in an enormous grey coat whom he had reluctantly admitted to the castle. She had been soaking wet from the storm raging outside, and was no doubt dripping water onto the silk carpet in the drawing room where he had instructed her to wait.

Cesario cursed beneath his breath. The only person he could think of who would dare to turn up at the Castello del

Falco uninvited was the journalist who had been hounding him recently and wanted to interview him about the accident which had claimed the lives of his wife and child. His jaw hardened. Perhaps it was to be expected that the press were fascinated by the reclusive billionaire owner of one of Italy's largest banks, but he resented any intrusion on his privacy and never spoke to journalists.

'The *signorina* introduced herself as Beth Granger.'

Teodoro's voice broke into Cesario's thoughts. It was not the name the journalist had given when she'd somehow managed to get hold of his private mobile phone number. But the name Beth Granger *was* familiar. He recalled that his PA had said an Englishwoman had phoned his office in Rome several times the previous week, asking to speak to him. 'She said she needs to talk to you about something important, but refused to give any more details,' Donata had informed him.

So maybe the journalist who had been badgering him was using a pseudonym? Or maybe Beth Granger was another member of the gutter press hoping to persuade him to drag up the past? Cesario was in no mood to find out.

'Inform this Ms Granger that I never see uninvited visitors at my private residence. Suggest that she contact Piras-Cossu's head office and explain her business to my secretary,' he instructed Teodoro. 'And then escort her from the castle.'

The butler hesitated. 'Ms Granger arrived by taxi, which subsequently left,' he explained, 'and it is raining.'

Cesario gave an impatient shrug. He had experienced the underhand tactics used by certain journalists too often to feel any sympathy. 'Then call another taxi. I want her off the premises immediately.'

With a stiff nod Teodoro turned and made his way back

down the sweeping staircase. Cesario glanced over the balcony at the guests milling about the ballroom. He wished the evening was over, but he had yet to make a speech, after which he would present a retirement gift to one of his executives and give an award to the Employee of the Year.

Duty took precedence over his personal feelings, he reminded himself. It was a lesson ingrained in him by his father and reinforced by his position as master of the Castello del Falco. The castle had been built by his ancestors in the thirteenth century; its history ran deep in his bones and the ancient greystone fortress was his bastion away from the scrutiny of the rest of the world. Duty drove Cesario to push thoughts of his son to the innermost recesses of his mind, and he squared his shoulders before striding down the stairs to rejoin his guests.

Beth was glad to be inside the castle out of the torrential rain. Her wool coat was soaked through to the lining, and she wondered if she could take it off without disturbing Sophie. It would be impossible, she realised, without first laying the baby down on the sofa and thereby risking waking her. She carefully shifted Sophie into the crook of one arm and tried to unfasten the top button, so that she could at least push the coat's hood back from her face. But after fumbling unsuccessfully for several minutes she gave up.

Surely Cesario Piras would not be much longer, she thought, feeling a flutter of trepidation at the prospect of meeting him. She glanced around the room to which the butler had escorted her before he had gone to inform the master of the Castello del Falco of her arrival. The plush jade-coloured carpet complemented the brocade curtains that were drawn across the windows. Two ornate lamps illuminated an exquisite tapestry hanging above the fire-place. But despite these decorations the room, with its bare stone walls, seemed as sombre and forbidding as the castle had looked from the outside when her taxi had pulled up in the courtyard.

Once again Beth cursed her fanciful imagination and tried to dismiss her unease. But as she stared down at the baby in her arms she prayed that Cesario Piras would be more welcoming than his home.

The door opened and she quickly looked up, her heart thudding with nervous expectation. But it was only the butler who walked back into the room.

Teodoro halted, and a flicker of surprise crossed his face when he saw that the visitor was holding a small baby. He had not noticed the child when he had admit-ted the woman into the castle. He was unaware that when Beth had climbed out of the taxi and hurried up the castle steps she had pulled her coat around Sophie to shield her from the rain.

Teodoro hesitated, and his gaze rested on the sleeping infant for a few seconds before he returned his attention to Beth. 'I am afraid the master is busy and cannot see you, *signorina*. Signor Piras suggests that you telephone his office in Rome and speak to his personal assistant, who oversees his business diary.'

'I *have* phoned his office—several times.'

Beth's heart plummeted. She had been doubtful about bringing Sophie to Sardinia, but Cesario Piras had refused to take her calls, and in desperation she had decided that the only option left to her was to travel to his home and hope he would agree to see her. It appeared that she had wasted her time—not to mention the cost of a flight from England that she could ill afford.

'I wish to talk to him about a personal matter,' she explained. 'Please…will you tell Mr Piras that I must see him urgently?'

The butler's impassive features did not alter. 'I am sorry, but the master has refused to see you.'

The pleading look in the young woman's eyes evoked a degree of sympathy in Teodoro, but he knew better than to disturb Cesario for a second time. Ms Granger's face was pale and tense beneath the hood of her coat. But he could not help her. The master of the Castello del Falco guarded his privacy as fiercely as his ancestors had guarded their mountain fortress, and Teodoro had no wish to incur Cesario's anger by disobeying an order.

'I will arrange for a taxi to come and collect you,' he told her. 'Please remain here until it arrives.'

'Wait…' Beth stared after the butler as he departed from the room, feeling a sense of helpless despair that her attempt to see Cesario Piras had failed. She had brought Sophie all this way for nothing. She bit her lip. Soon the baby would wake and need to be fed, but the journey back down to the hotel where she was staying in Oliena would take at least half an hour. She would have to give Sophie a bottle of milk in the taxi, Beth thought heavily, unless she could persuade the butler to allow her to feed her here at the castle.

She hurried out of the room after him, but found the entrance hall empty. As she stood wondering what to do a set of double doors at the far end of the hall suddenly swung open and a maid appeared, carrying a tray of empty glasses. Beth took a step forward, but before she could speak the maid had disappeared through another door.

The double doors remained open, and beyond them Beth saw a crowd of people: men in dinner suits and women wearing ballgowns in rainbow hues of silk and satin. Waiters in white jackets, bearing trays of drinks and canapés, wove skilfully among the throng of guests, and the sound of music and voices mingled to form a discordant melody.

A party! Beth felt a spurt of anger. Cesario Piras had refused to see her because he was *busy* enjoying himself at a party. He hadn't even given her a chance to explain the reason for her visit. She looked down at Sophie's tiny face and her heart turned over at the sight of the baby's long, dark eyelashes resting on her pink cheeks. Fierce determination swept through her. She had promised Mel she would find Cesario Piras, and now that she was here at his castle she was *not* going to leave without speaking to him.

Without waiting to reconsider her decision, she walked swiftly across the entrance hall. But her nerve faltered and she hesitated in the doorway of the vast room where the party was taking place. The walls here were not bare stone but dark wood panels that gleamed softly in the light cast from the huge chandeliers above. Elegant pillars lined either side of the room, soaring up to support an arched ceiling decorated with exquisite murals.

Beth wished the room was empty, so that she could appreciate its architecture and soak up its history. She possessed a vivid imagination and pictured knights in armour and an age of chivalry that had long since passed. But the room was full of people, and as she moved forward she was conscious of heads turning and curious glances cast in her direction from many of the party guests.

The buzz of chatter faded as people stepped back to allow her to continue. The music had stopped. Ahead of her a figure strode onto a raised platform at the far end of the room. It seemed that he intended to address the guests, but he halted when he caught sight of Beth and even from a distance she could sense his surprise.

How long was this room? Beth wondered frantically. The black-and-white chequered marble floor seemed to go on for ever, and she wondered if she would ever reach the end of it. The silence and the stares made her feel agonisingly self-conscious. Her heart was thudding beneath her ribs but she could not turn back now. Something about the arrogant stance and the air of authority of the man on the dais made her certain that he was the man Mel had asked her to find.

Santa Madre! Cesario stared in disbelief at the woman walking towards him. At least he assumed it was a woman. It was difficult to tell the identity of the figure beneath the huge grey coat with its hood that half concealed the wearer's face. But this could only be the visitor whom Teodoro had explained had arrived at the castle a short while ago and demanded to see him.

What Teodoro had failed to mention was that Beth Granger was not alone. The baby in her arms could not be more than a couple of months old, Cesario estimated. The infant was wrapped in a shawl, but a tuft of silky dark hair was visible. He inhaled sharply, struck by poignant memories of his son when he had been newborn.

He did not know who the woman was, but he wanted her to leave, he thought grimly. Tonight he was impatient for everyone to be gone so that he could be alone with his memories.

Teodoro burst into the ballroom, looking uncharacteristically harassed as he hurried towards the dais. 'Signor

Piras, I apologise. I was arranging transport for the *signorina…*'

'It's all right, Teodoro.' Cesario held up a hand to silence the butler. 'I will deal with our unexpected visitor.'

The woman had faltered for a moment when Teodoro had spoken, but now she quickened her pace. Cesario jumped down from the dais and in two strides stood in front of her.

'I hope you have an excellent reason for gatecrashing my party, Ms Granger,' he said coldly. 'You have thirty seconds to explain why you are here before I order my staff to escort you from my home.'

Forced to an abrupt halt, Beth opened her mouth to speak. But her brain seemed to have stopped functioning and she was bereft of words. She had never appreciated the meaning of the word *dumbstruck* until now, she acknowledged dazedly. She had been relieved when the butler had confirmed that the man standing in front of her was indeed Cesario Piras. But she was unprepared for her reaction to him.

He towered over her, so that she was forced to tilt her head to study his face. Her eyes were drawn to the jagged scar which slashed across his left cheek. She could not deny that it marred his otherwise perfect features, causing his eyelid to droop fractionally and zig-zagging over his smooth olive skin to the corner of his mouth. But the disfigurement did not lessen the impact of his raw sexual magnetism; rather, it gave him the look of a pirate, or a knight from ancient times.

He was nothing like Beth had imagined a banker would be. His hair was jet-black and fell in a tousled mane almost to his shoulders. The dark stubble shading his jaw was dangerously sexy, and his razor-sharp cheekbones and aquiline nose gave him an autocratic appearance. But it was his eyes that trapped her gaze. Slate-grey, and as hard as granite, they regarded her intently from beneath heavy brows and gave Beth the unnerving feeling that he could see into her very soul.

He was waiting for her reply. She sensed that everyone in the room was waiting, and the silence pressed on her eardrums. She licked her suddenly dry lips. 'I'm sorry for my intrusion, but I need to speak with you, Mr Piras...' Conscious of the curious stares of the party guests she added, 'Alone.'

His frown deepened, his expression so forbidding that Beth instinctively tightened her arms around Sophie.

'How dare you come here uninvited and disturb my privacy?'

He spoke in perfect English but with a strong accent. His voice was deep and husky, and caused tiny pinpricks of sensation to dart across Beth's skin.

In the lengthening silence Cesario studied the woman. If she had been alone he would have had no compunction in ordering his staff to remove her from the castle. Certainly if Beth Granger was a journalist he had every right to throw her out. But he could not deny he was curious about why she had brought a baby out on such a wet and wild night.

His eyes were drawn to the child in her arms and his gut clenched. Once he had held his son and marvelled at the perfection of his tiny features. Once he had cradled Nicolo against his heart and promised to protect him. His failure to keep his promise would haunt him for the rest of his life.

A discreet cough broke into his thoughts, dragging him back to the present. He glanced around the crowded ballroom. Three hundred of Piras-Cossu's senior staff had been invited to the party and all of them, it seemed, were riveted by the scene unfolding in front of them.

'Come with me,' he ordered the woman abruptly. 'Teodoro, tell the band to continue playing.'

Beth hurried after Cesario Piras as he strode across the room and disappeared through an arched doorway. She followed him into what seemed to be a small store-room, where bottles of wine and champagne were stored on shelves that lined the walls from floor to ceiling. The thud of the door closing made her spin round and she eyed him warily, even more conscious of his height and impos-ing presence in the confined space.

He did not bother to conceal his impatience. 'State your business, Ms Granger. Why have you come here? I hope for your sake you are not a member of the press,' he added harshly.

Startled, Beth quickly shook her head. No... I'm not... I...' Her voice trailed away. She had rehearsed this mo-ment over and over in her mind, but now that it was here for real she was beset with doubts. It did not help that Cesario Piras was so formidable. Maybe she should say nothing and take Sophie back to England, she thought, un-consciously gnawing on her bottom lip as she struggled to make a decision. But she had given her word to Mel.

She lifted her eyes to meet his hard grey gaze and felt her heart slam against her ribcage. A medieval castle suited him perfectly, she thought ruefully. He exuded an air of power and authority, and she sensed that he was as strong and uncompromising as the granite walls of his castle.

Perhaps he was a sorcerer who had trapped her in his spell? She could not look away from him, and in that mo-ment something happened—something unexpected and impossible to explain. She felt a sharp pain beneath her ribs, as if an arrow had pierced her heart. *Don't be ridiculous*, she silently berated herself. How could she feel a connection to a complete stranger? Especially a stranger who was staring at her with grim impatience etched onto his scarred face.

She looked down at Sophie and took a deep breath. 'I have come, because the child I am holding is yours, Mr Piras,' she said quietly.

CHAPTER TWO

Was this some kind of obscene joke? Cesario wondered savagely. What did this unknown woman who kept her face hidden beneath the hood of her coat mean?

'Explain yourself,' he ordered. 'I do not have a child.' The words scraped a raw wound inside him.

'Sophie is your baby. She was conceived on this night a year ago.'

With an impatient oath Cesario shot out an arm and wrenched Beth Granger's hood back from her face, sending a button flying in the process.

He did not recognise her.

He had slept with a few women since he had been widowed, but she was not one of them. Anger seared him. He was aware that his wealth meant that he could be targeted by unscrupulous women hoping to make easy money by claiming that he had fathered them a child. But this was ridiculous; he had never laid eyes on Beth Granger before. Perhaps she had hoped to convince the lawyers that it had been an immaculate conception? he thought sardonically.

He subjected her to a slow, deliberate appraisal, taking in her tangled mousy hair and the drab, shapeless coat that looked as though she had borrowed it from a street beggar.

'I think not, Ms Granger,' he drawled mockingly.

'Undoubtedly I would remember if *you* had ever shared my bed.'

Heat scalded Beth's cheeks. Cesario Piras's meaning was humiliatingly clear. She was far too unattractive ever to have caught his eye. No doubt he was only interested in gorgeous women like Mel had been. Blonde, beautiful Mel had had men lusting after her since high school, and it was not surprising that she had attracted the attention of a billionaire banker.

Compared to her best friend, Beth had always felt like an ugly duckling—and never more so than at this moment, when she was bedraggled and exhausted, wearing a coat she had bought from a charity shop which was several sizes too big. Recalling the scornful glances of the party guests when she had walked into the ballroom, she had a sudden flashback to when she was sixteen and had attended the school prom in a dress that the manager of the care home had lent her. Mrs Clarke had said she looked lovely, but of course she hadn't. She had looked what she was: a girl with no parents and no money, in a dress that didn't belong to her.

Sophie would never suffer that kind of humiliation, Beth vowed fiercely. Not if she could help it. She loved the baby with all her heart, but she knew from bitter experience the importance of money. She wanted Sophie to have all the things she had never had: nice clothes, a good education, the confidence that came with feeling that you were somebody rather than a nobody.

Carefully cradling the baby in one arm, she delved into the pocket of her coat and withdrew a photograph.

'Sophie is not my child.'

She lifted her chin to meet Cesario's hard stare and held out the photo to him. 'This is her mother—Melanie

Stewart. Mel attended a party in London exactly a year ago. It was a big event, to celebrate something to do with Piras-Cossu taking over an English bank. I don't know the details. But Mel met you at the party and later you invited her up to your hotel room. It was a one-night stand. She never even knew your name. But she fell pregnant that night with your baby.'

'What utter nonsense,' Cesario snapped witheringly. 'I don't appreciate having my time wasted, Ms Granger.'

Her story was so unbelievable it was almost laughable, but he was not amused. He plucked the photograph from Beth's fingers and glanced down at the image of a voluptuous blonde. The picture meant nothing to him. He did not remember the woman. But then he did not remember much at all about the party at the exclusive Heskeath Hotel in Mayfair a year ago, his conscience taunted him.

It had been his duty to attend the reception, organised by the managing director of the new UK subsidiary of the Piras-Cossu Bank. But that night, just as tonight, Cesario's thoughts had been with his son. For a couple of hours he'd forced himself to make polite small-talk, but he'd spent the latter part of the evening at the bar, drowning his emotions in neat bourbon.

There might have been a woman. He frowned as fractured memories forced their way into his mind. He vaguely remembered a blonde at the bar. He recalled buying her a drink, and he had a hazy memory of dancing with her.

Shock ricocheted through him. *Could* there be any truth in Beth Granger's story? Could he have slept with this Melanie Stewart and have no memory of it? He'd been so drunk that it would have been a miracle if he had managed to perform, let alone father a child, he thought derisively. A miracle—but he could not discount the possibility.

Conflicting emotions surged through him: disbelief, followed by self-disgust that he might have had sex with the woman in the photograph and yet retain no knowledge of her or what had taken place between them. He could not profess that he lived like a monk. He'd had one-night stands occasionally, but they had been a mutual exchange of sexual pleasure—not a drunken fumble he had no memory of and which, if this woman Beth Granger could be believed, had resulted in a child—*his* child.

His eyes were drawn to the baby. A girl—named Sophie. *Inferno! Was she his daughter?* He felt a pain in his gut, an ache of longing for the child he had lost. Beth Granger could be lying, he reminded himself. For a start, he did not understand why *she* had brought the baby to Sardinia. Where was the child's mother?

A tiny cry broke from the baby as she began to wake.

'She's due a feed,' Beth explained, looking at him anxiously. 'I need to make up her formula.'

The sound of the child's cry pierced Cesario's soul. He remembered the first cry his son had given as he had entered the world, and he closed his eyes for a few seconds, praying that when he opened them again he would find that he had imagined the woman and the baby.

She was still there, her attention focused on the child that she was now rocking in her arms. *The baby could not be his.* His mind refused to accept such an astounding idea. But he realised that he could not send Beth Granger away without listening to what she had to say.

Cesario withdrew his phone from his jacket and pressed a number on the keypad. Almost instantly there was a knock on the door and the butler entered the room.

'Escort Ms Granger to the library and ensure that she

has everything she requires,' he instructed Teodoro. 'I will join her shortly.'

The butler dipped his head in acknowledgement. 'Please follow me, Signorina Granger.'

Feeling horribly self-conscious, Beth walked back through the great hall after the butler and expelled a sigh of relief when he closed the doors behind them and she was no longer the subject of dozens of curious glances. Her legs felt shaky. She gave a rueful grimace as she acknowledged that her encounter with the master of the Castello del Falco had left her feeling as limp as a wrung-out rag.

He was so intimidating. *And so ruggedly handsome*, a little voice in her head whispered. Even with that shocking scar. She wondered what had happened to him. How had he come by such a terrible injury? But, recalling his steel-hard gaze, she knew she would never have the courage to ask.

The taxi driver had carried Sophie's pushchair and nappy bag into the castle and left them on the porch, she explained to Teodoro when he ushered her into the library. While he went to fetch them she laid the now wide-awake Sophie on the rug, and was rewarded with a winsome smile that melted her heart.

'You are too cute,' she told the baby girl softly. At the sound of her voice Sophie chuckled and kicked her legs. But Beth knew from experience that Sophie's smiles would quickly turn to a demanding cry if she was not fed soon. Taking responsibility for her best friend's baby had been a steep learning curve, she acknowledged ruefully. But never once, not even on the nights when Sophie had simply refused to sleep and cried for hours, had she regretted that Mel had appointed her as the baby's guardian.

Even though Mel's wishes had been clearly stated in her

will, Beth had had to go through several nerve-racking interviews with Social Services before she had been deemed suitable to have Sophie and allowed to take her home from the hospital. But none of that mattered. The important thing was that Sophie would not grow up in a children's home, as her mother and Beth had both done.

'Your mummy wanted me to look after you, and be a mum to you in her place,' she whispered to Sophie. 'I will always love you, and I'll never let anyone take you away from me. It's just you and me, my angel.'

But that wasn't quite true. The thought struck Beth as she shrugged out of her coat. There was also Sophie's father to consider. Her stomach muscles tightened involuntarily as she wondered how long it would be before Cesario Piras appeared. She could not forget those moments in the ballroom when he had studied her with unconcealed contempt, as if she was something unpleasant that had crawled out from beneath a stone. She knew perfectly well that she was plain, and usually she did not care overmuch about her lack of looks, but for some reason Cesario's dismissive expression had made her wish that she was beautiful and glamorous—like so many of his female party guests.

She sighed. There was no point wanting to be something she was never going to be, she told herself firmly. But she could at least make sure that she looked tidy and presentable. A glance in the mirror above the fireplace confirmed that her hair was no longer secured in a neat chignon but was hanging in damp rats' tails around her face. There was no time to tie it up again when Sophie needed her nappy changed, and so she quickly removed the last of the pins and pulled a comb through her hair before she knelt down on the rug to attend to the baby.

* * *

Cesario strode across the entrance hall towards the library, his tension evident in the rigid set of his jaw. He had delegated to his chief executive the task of making a speech to the guests, and now he was intent on getting to the bottom of Beth Granger's extraordinary story. His initial shock at her startling claim that he was the father of the child she had brought to the castle had been replaced by a healthy dose of common sense. There were numerous flaws in her story and many questions that he wanted answered before he would give her claim any credence.

It was even possible that she was gold-digger who had invented her incredible tale to try and extort money out of him, he thought darkly. He'd had experience of a confidence trickster once before. Some years ago a young man had declared that he was Orsino Piras's illegitimate son and was entitled to a share of the Piras fortune. DNA evidence had disproved the claim, but Cesario had never believed there was any truth in it. His father had been a cold, remote man, and his only mistress had been the bank which had now been owned by the Piras family for five generations.

He pushed open the library door and hesitated on the threshold of the room, his eyes drawn to the young woman who was sitting on the sofa cradling the baby in her arms. Without her coat Beth Granger was much slimmer than his first impression of her. She was rather too slender for his tastes, he mused, noting her small, high breasts and the fragile line of her collarbone visible where the top couple of buttons of her blouse were undone.

Her grey skirt and navy blouse looked as though they had been bought from a bargain store, and her flat black shoes were scuffed and well-worn. But, although her clothes were unflattering, she possessed a quiet grace that he found unexpectedly appealing. She was not beautiful in a conventional sense, Cesario observed. But her heart-shaped face, slightly upturned nose and full mouth held a certain charm, and now that her hair was loose he saw that it was a pale golden-brown, gleaming like silk in the light from the lamp and falling to halfway down her back.

He was surprised by a compelling desire to touch her hair and feel its softness against his skin. He immediately dismissed the thought and walked into the room, noting the quick, nervous glance she darted at him. For a few seconds his gaze locked with a pair of vivid green eyes fringed by hazel lashes, before she returned her attention to the baby she was feeding from a bottle.

Images from the past flooded his mind. He remembered being in the nursery with Raffaella, watching her feeding Nicolo. Their love for their son had been the one thing they had shared; the only bond between two people whose marriage had in no way been a love-match.

For him, marriage to Raffaella Cossu had ensured the merger of the Piras and Cossu banks and made him one of the most powerful men in Italy. Driven by ambition, he had considered a marriage of convenience a small price to pay—or so he had believed, Cesario thought grimly. He had liked Raffaella well enough, and falling in love had never been on his agenda. Experience had taught him that love was an overrated emotion—one which frequently led to pain and disappointment.

He had loved his mother once—adored her. But when he was seven years old she had left his father for her lover and he had never seen her or spoken to her again.

'Stop snivelling like a baby,' his father had told him when he had found him crying in his room. 'Do not waste your tears on a woman. You will find as you grow older

*that there are always plenty more, especially for a man
who has wealth and power.'*

Power was the golden grail, Cesario mused cynically.
For the Cossu family their lack of a son to inherit their
bank had led them to seek a merger with the Piras bank
by marrying off their daughter to Cesario. Raffaella had
obeyed her parents' wishes, or perhaps been coerced—
Cesario had never known. And eighteen months after their
marriage she had dutifully given him an heir.

All would have been well if she had not fallen in love
with another man. Love had blown everything apart.
Raffaella's decision to leave her marriage to be with her
lover, and Cesario's determination to keep his son—whom
he had loved more than he had known it was possible
to love another human being—had resulted in a bitter
confrontation, and ultimately in the accident which had
claimed Raffaella and Nicolo's lives.

A nerve jumped in Cesario's cheek. He had become
adept at blocking out painful memories, and his expression was shuttered as he stood in front of the fireplace and
stared at the woman whose arrival at the castle had such
disturbing implications.

Sophie had finished her feed, and when Beth sat her
upright on her lap she looked about her with wide-eyed
curiosity. With a mass of silky black hair and dark brown
eyes fringed by impossibly long lashes, the child was as
pretty as a doll, Cesario noted, finding it impossible to
tear his gaze from her.

'When was she born?' he demanded abruptly.

'The twenty-eighth of October.'

He stiffened at Beth's reply and his expression became
steely. 'In that case she cannot be my child. If Sophie was
conceived this time last year she would have been due in

December. I'll be frank with you. I have no recollection of sleeping with the woman in the photograph, but I'd had a lot to drink and I cannot be certain that I did not invite her back to my room. But Melanie Stewart must have already been pregnant if she gave birth seven months later.' His tone became mocking. 'You should have worked out the maths before you embarked on your little game, Ms Granger.'

'I'm not playing a game,' Beth said sharply, stung by his sarcasm. 'Sophie was born nearly two months premature. That's why she's small for a four-month-old baby.' She flushed at Cesario's disbelieving look. 'It's the truth. Mel was ill and the doctors had to deliver Sophie early.'

'So where is Melanie Stewart now? Why isn't she caring for her daughter? And who, exactly, are you?'

'Mel is dead.' Beth's voice caught in her throat as she stared at Sophie and felt a pang of grief for her friend, who had only seen her baby a few times before she had died. It still seemed impossible that Mel was gone. She had always been the strong one out of the two of them, the daring one, who had teased Beth for being a timid mouse and protected her from the school bullies with her acid tongue and fiery temper.

She realised that Cesario was waiting for her to continue, and took a ragged breath. 'Last autumn there was a flu epidemic in England that was especially serious for pregnant women. Mel thought she just had a cold, but within two days she was in Intensive Care, fighting for her life. The doctors decided to deliver Sophie early to give mother and baby a chance. But Sophie was tiny; she only weighed three pounds and was placed in the special care baby unit.'

Tears choked her as she remembered watching Sophie

through the clear plastic walls of the incubator, willing the tiny scrap of humanity to live. 'For a while Mel rallied and things looked optimistic. She was even able to hold Sophie once, for a few minutes. But a few days later she died suddenly. The doctor said the flu virus had put too much strain on her heart.'

Beth blinked hard to dispel her tears. She finally had Cesario's attention, and she needed to convince him that he had a responsibility towards Sophie. She swallowed and forced herself to continue.

'A few days before her death Mel told me she had recognised your photo in a newspaper. The paper had printed your name, and she realised that the man she had slept with at the party in London was Cesario Piras, and that you were Sophie's father. I had already agreed that if anything happened to Mel I would look after Sophie. Mel made me promise that if she died I would try to find you and let you know you had a daughter.'

Cesario was silent while he absorbed the information Beth had given him. She must know it would be easy enough to verify her story, and therefore it was unlikely she was lying. But even if what she had said was true, it did not prove that the child on her lap was his.

If only he could remember the events at that party in London a year ago. But that night he had turned to drink to banish the demons that haunted him, to silence for a few hours the voice in his head that insisted *he* had been partially responsible for Nicolo's death.

His hard features revealed nothing of his thoughts. 'What part do you play in this, Ms Granger? Why did you agree to take care of Ms Stewart's child? Why aren't her family involved?'

'Mel didn't have any family. Her parents died when

she was young and she grew up in care—as I did, after my mother died. We met in a children's home and became friends.' Once again Beth's voice was husky. 'When Mel found out she was pregnant I promised I would help her bring up the baby. After she died I learned that she had named me as Sophie's legal guardian.'

Cesario swung around and rested his arm along the mantelpiece, staring at the black empty grate. He should have asked one of the staff to light a fire, he thought heavily. He could hear the rain still beating against the walls of the castle. Perhaps the room was too chilly for a small baby.

He remembered how in the first weeks after Nicolo had been born he had felt awed by the responsibility of caring for a new life. His little son had seemed so vulnerable that Cesario had found himself constantly checking on him, and he had demanded that fires be lit in every room in the castle so that the baby was not exposed to any cold draughts.

He had never expected to see another baby at the Castello del Falco. Four years ago he had vowed never to marry again, or have another child. It was inconceivable that anyone could ever replace Nicolo in his heart. Yet, unbelievably, he was now faced with the possibility that he had a daughter who had been conceived on the anniversary of the date he had lost his son. Was it a bizarre twist of fate? he wondered. Or a fabrication invented by a woman who claimed she had been asked by the child's mother to find him? There was only one way to establish the truth.

'I will arrange for a DNA test to be done,' he said abruptly. 'I admit I was drunk at the party in London a year ago, but I find it hard to believe that I slept with your friend and have no recollection of it.'

The idea that he could have been so out of control that he'd unknowingly had sex with a woman he'd picked up in a bar did not sit comfortably with Cesario.

'However,' he continued roughly, 'I accept that it *is* a possibility, and therefore a paternity test is necessary. Until it can be done, and the results obtained, you and the baby will stay here at the Castello del Falco.'

Beth felt a spurt of shock—partly at the arrogance of the man standing a few feet from her and partly at the implication of his words. Stay here? In this grim, grey castle? With its equally forbidding owner? The idea sent a shiver through her.

'Oh, no, that's not necessary,' she explained quickly. 'I expected you would want a DNA test, so I booked a room at a hotel in Oliena for three days. Once the test has been done I'll take Sophie back to England and wait there for the results.'

She did not add that she was sure the test would prove Cesario *was* the man Mel had slept with. Mel had been certain she had recognised him in the newspaper.

You must find Cesario Piras and demand financial help for Sophie, she had said in the note she had left for Beth.

Mel must have sensed that she was not going to live, Beth thought sadly. And in her last days she had attempted to arrange some measure of security for her daughter by asking Beth to search for the man she'd believed was Sophie's father.

Cesario frowned. 'It makes more sense for you and the child to stay here until we know for sure whether or not she is mine.'

His gaze was drawn to the baby, and he felt as though

he had been kicked in the gut when she turned her head and stared at him with her huge dark eyes. She was beautiful—almost as beautiful as his son had been. Was it his imagination, or did she bear a resemblance to Nicolo? *Dio*, was she his?

The idea was so shocking that he could not begin to assimilate how he felt about it. But one thing struck him forcibly. *If* Sophie was his daughter she deserved his care and protection. He could not at this point contemplate the notion that she would also deserve his love. Losing Nicolo had almost destroyed him, and the idea of loving another child evoked a host of feelings inside him. The strongest of which, he admitted grimly, was fear. Experience had taught him that love was a bittersweet emotion. It would be better if Sophie was not his child, but until he knew the truth he wanted her to remain here at the castle.

That meant that for now, at least, Beth Granger would have to stay too. He wasn't sure what to make of her. On the face of it her apparent willingness to take on her friend's child seemed amazingly altruistic. She was young—he guessed in her early twenties—and from her shabby clothes it was safe to assume that she did not have much money. Could he believe that she had agreed to act as guardian to another woman's child out of the kindness of her heart?

'Mr Piras, there's really no need for you to go to any trouble—especially tonight, when you are busy with your party,' Beth said a little desperately. 'The hotel has provided a cot for Sophie, and I left our luggage there.'

'I'll send one of my staff to collect your things and bring them back to the castle.' Cesario's eyes narrowed when Beth looked about to argue. 'It is still raining heavily. Surely you cannot think it a good idea to take a baby out in such weather? I am inviting you and Sophie to stay here as my guests.' He paused, and then added, 'Under the circumstances, I think we should drop formalities and use our respective Christian names.'

He was so intimidating that she could not imagine she would ever feel confident enough to use his first name, Beth thought wryly. Skirting around the issue of how to address him, she focused on a far more important problem. 'But where will Sophie sleep? I have her buggy with me, but although she naps in it during the day it's not suitable for her to sleep in all night.'

'The castle has a nursery which is fully equipped with everything you might need.'

It was a long time since he had visited the room which had once been his son's, and for a moment Cesario struggled with the idea of allowing another child to sleep in the antique hand-carved cot that Nicolo had slept in until only a few months before his death, when he had moved into a 'big bed'. But he could not deny a baby a safe place to sleep, he reminded himself.

'I don't want to be a nuisance,' Beth mumbled, her heart sinking as she acknowledged she could offer no other reason for her and Sophie not to stay at Cesario's home. She could hear the wind howling around the castle turrets, and the rain hammering against the windows sounded even heavier than when she had arrived. For Sophie's sake it would be better to remain here, but she wished the enigmatic master of the Castello del Falco did not have such a strange effect on her.

Throughout their conversation she had been intensely aware of him. Her eyes seemed to have a magnetic attraction to his tall, imposing figure as he leaned against the fireplace. His close-fitting black trousers moulded his muscular thighs, and his white shirt was made of such fine silk that she could see the faint shadow of dark chest hairs beneath it.

She lifted her head and flushed when she met his hooded gaze, embarrassed that he had caught her staring at him. He was probably used to women being fascinated by him, she thought ruefully. The livid scar on his cheek did not detract from his incredible good-looks. Ruggedly handsome, he possessed a dark, smouldering sensuality which evoked a curious sensation in the pit of her stomach—an ache of longing for something she did not understand but that she sensed this man, with his earthy virility, could appease.

What was the matter with her? she asked herself impatiently, as a shockingly vivid image came into her mind of being kissed by Cesario Piras. She could not help wondering what it would be like to be crushed against his broad chest and feel his lips on hers. She knew she was sexually naive for a woman of nearly twenty-four, but after her father had walked out when she was a child—leaving her and her seriously ill mother to fend for themselves—she had found it hard to trust any man. She had dated a few men, but nothing had ever been serious and she'd never felt any desire to take things further than a goodnight kiss at the end of an evening.

She sensed instinctively that Cesario would want more than a few chaste kisses. He would be passionate and demanding, and undoubtedly a skilled lover…

Horrified by her wanton thoughts, she hastily sought to break the silence that stretched between them. 'Hopefully it won't take long to arrange the test. We'll probably only need to stay for a few days.'

Cesario shrugged. 'I wish for you to remain here until

the results of the test are known, which I believe can take a week or more.'

He could not take his eyes off the baby. He felt a sense of incredulity that she might possibly be his, but if she was then there was no question he would deny responsibility for her.

'If it is proved that Sophie is my child, she will live with me here at the castle,' he stated decisively.

'Live here!' Shock, followed almost immediately by a sense of wild panic paralysed Beth's vocal cords so that her voice emerged as a faint gasp.

'Where else would she live?' Cesario queried, sounding surprised by her reaction. 'If Sophie is a Piras, then the Castello del Falco is her home and her heritage.'

'But I am Sophie's legal guardian. I promised Mel I would be a mother to her baby. And I live in Hackney,' Beth added desperately, clutching Sophie tightly to her, as if she feared Cesario would snatch the baby from her arms.

'If I am her father she will have no need of a guardian.'

Cesario's eyes narrowed speculatively on Beth's tense face.

'You clearly went to a lot of trouble to find me,' he said after a moment, 'and you were prepared for Sophie to undergo a DNA test. What do you expect me to do if it is established that she is my child? Surely you do not think I would simply allow you to take her back to England?'

'I…' Beth floundered, not knowing how to answer. The truth was she had assumed that Cesario Piras would want nothing to do with his daughter. Perhaps the fact that she had been abandoned by her own father had made her cynical. But a man who had had casual sex and carelessly did not use protection did not seem likely to accept responsibility for the baby who had resulted from a one-night stand. Cesario hadn't even told Mel his name, she thought disgustedly. If it hadn't been for the newspaper photo the identity of Sophie's father would have for ever been a mystery.

'It didn't occur to me that you might want to be involved with your baby,' she admitted.

'Then why go to the effort of tracking me down?'

Cesario's granite stare was so unnerving that Beth hurriedly looked away from him. 'I hoped to persuade you to make a financial settlement for Sophie,' she muttered.

She felt her face flood with colour. The statement sounded so cold-blooded, but she was innately honest and could not deny the truth. The idea of asking for money was abhorrent to her, but the harsh reality was that she could not afford to bring up Sophie on the low wage she earned from her cleaning job. She was a qualified nanny, but after she'd been unfairly sacked from her last position she had lost confidence and became wary of looking for another placement. Even if she could find a better job, the cost of childcare, rent and bills would leave nothing for all the things she wanted Sophie to have: music lessons, ballet classes, *new* clothes rather than hand-me-downs—all the things she had longed for when she had been a child.

The atmosphere in the library had become tangibly tense. Beth darted Cesario a nervous glance and discovered that his granite gaze had turned to steel: cold and hard and edged with a mocking contempt that caused her stomach to cramp.

'So you want money?'

'For Sophie,' she insisted sharply, stung by his scornful tone. 'If it is proved that she is your child, then it's only fair that you should contribute towards her upbringing.'

'And, as her legal guardian, you assumed *you* would have control of any allowance I might provide.' His lip curled. 'I understand now why agreeing to bring up your friend's daughter after you had learned that Sophie's possible father was a billionaire was such an attractive proposition,' Cesario drawled.

'It had nothing to do with that,' Beth denied hotly, appalled by the implication. 'What a horrible thing to suggest. My only consideration is for Sophie. I love her—and I loved Mel,' she said thickly. 'We were best friends. More like sisters. I didn't expect her to die, but she did. I intend to keep the promise I made to her to take her place as Sophie's mother, but I don't think it is unreasonable to ask for a little financial assistance so that I can give Sophie a happy childhood.'

'If Sophie is my child then she will want for nothing,' Cesario said harshly. 'But you will be superfluous. You will no longer be required to act as her guardian and you'll be free to return to England.'

Fear gripped Beth. 'What do you mean—superfluous?' she asked shakily. 'I've cared for Sophie since the day she was born. I took her home from the hospital. One day, when she's older, I will tell her about her real mother, but for now I'm the only mother she knows and nothing on this earth could persuade me to give her up.'

Cesario was almost convinced that the tremor of emotion in her voice was genuine. Almost—but not quite. He could not forget the fact that Beth had sought him out because she wanted a financial settlement for her friend's child. He was still stunned by the possibility that Sophie might be his, but if she *was* then he had a duty towards her, and there was no question in his mind that she should do anything other than live in Sardinia with him.

As for Beth Granger… To his annoyance his gaze was drawn to her face and he felt an unbidden flicker of compassion when he noted the shimmer of tears in her green eyes. For a heartbeat they stared at one another, before she dropped her head and a swathe of her gleaming brown hair fell across her cheek.

A hot, fierce throb of desire flared in Cesario's groin, taking him by surprise so that he drew a sharp breath. For a few crazy seconds he imagined leaning down and slanting his lips over Beth's, tracing their moist softness with his tongue.

The thoughts in his head were totally inappropriate, he told himself angrily. Fighting a strong urge to reach out and tuck the silky strands of her hair behind her ear, he strode over to the door.

'A discussion on the child's future is premature until a DNA test has been done,' he said coolly. 'Until then I hope you will be comfortable at the Castello del Falco. I will instruct my staff to prepare the nursery. Teodoro will escort you upstairs and ensure you have everything you need. But now I must ask you to excuse me while I return to my guests.'

CHAPTER THREE

SHE needed to leave the castle immediately, get back to Oliena, arrange a transfer to the airport and book the next flight back to England. If she disappeared now Cesario would never be able find her. And without a paternity test there would be no risk of him trying to take Sophie away from her.

Beth's head was spinning with frantic thoughts, but she forced a smile for Cesario's butler as he ushered her out of the library and motioned that she should follow him up the stairs.

'There's been a change of plan. I've decided to return to my hotel tonight,' she told him in a falsely bright tone. 'There's no need for anyone to go all the way down to Oliena to collect my things. If you could just call me a taxi, I'll leave now while the baby has fallen back to sleep.'

Teodoro's inscrutable expression did not alter. 'A member of staff has already been dispatched to your hotel and will return with your luggage shortly. Signor Piras gave orders for the nursery to be made ready for the infant. If you would like to follow me, I will escort you there.'

Without another word he resumed his unhurried pace towards the ornately carved oak staircase which wound up to the upper floors of the castle. She was trapped, Beth realised fearfully. The taxi driver who had brought her here had only spoken a few words of English and she did not speak Italian. Even if she could find a phone number for a taxi firm her chances of making herself understood were minimal.

But the thought of staying at the castle made her stomach churn with nervous tension. When she had made the trip to Sardinia it hadn't crossed her mind that Cesario would *want* his baby. Maybe she had been wrong to assume that every man was as unreliable as her father, she thought heavily. She had expected Cesario to argue against having a DNA test. And if it had been proved that he *was* Sophie's father the most she had hoped for was that he would offer her a small allowance to help with the cost of bringing up his child.

Reluctantly acknowledging that she had no choice, Beth followed the butler up the stairs. Sophie was hers, she assured herself. Mel had appointed her as the baby's guardian. But would a court decide that Sophie's father had more right to bring her up than a guardian? She paused as a wave of dizziness swept over her and grabbed the banister rail for support. Her legs felt wobbly and she could not seem to draw enough oxygen into her lungs.

It was the same feeling she'd experienced a few times before, when she'd had to climb the five flights of stairs up to her flat because the lift in the tower block had been vandalised yet again. She took a deep breath and forced herself to calm down. There was no point in worrying about anything at the moment. Nothing could be decided until the results of the DNA test were known.

The nursery was at the end of a long passageway on the second floor. Beth had guessed that it would simply be a guest bedroom furnished with a cot, for the use of any visitors to the castle with a baby. She certainly had not expected *this*, she thought in astonishment when Teodoro ushered her into the room.

Spacious and airy, the room was painted a delicate primrose-yellow which complemented the pale oak furniture. A beautiful antique cot stood in the centre of the room and a maid was adjusting the exquisite cream lace bedding. She looked round when Beth entered the room and stared curiously at Sophie, before Teodoro spoke to her in Italian and she quickly left the room.

'Carlotta will bring you anything you need. Just pull on this rope here to call her,' he explained to Beth.

'Thank you.' She walked slowly across the cream velvet carpet and paused in front of a wooden rocking horse. She had seen pictures of luxurious nurseries like this one in glossy magazines featuring houses owned by wealthy celebrities. Everything here was the finest quality. But this room had not been designed as a showpiece. She sensed that love had gone into the creation of this nursery, and as she looked down at Sophie, who was asleep in her arms, an unexpected feeling of peace swept over her.

'It's a beautiful room,' she said softly. Something about the nursery puzzled her. Maybe it was simply her imagination, but she felt a presence that she could not explain. She glanced at the butler. 'It feels as though a child used to sleep here not that long ago.'

'It was Signor Piras's son's room.'

Beth could not hide her shock. *His son!* 'So, is Mr Piras married? Do his wife and son live at the castle?'

'Not any longer.' Teodoro gave her a brief nod. 'If there is nothing else, *signorina*, then I will leave you. The door over there leads to an adjoining bedroom, which has been prepared for you. I will have your bags sent up as soon as they arrive.'

Evidently the subject of Cesario's wife and child was not something the butler was prepared to discuss, but Beth had dozens of questions she longed to ask and felt a surge of frustration as Teodoro departed from the nursery. She wished she had been able to discover more about Cesario before she'd left England. He was the head of one of Italy's largest banks and she had expected to find a detailed profile about him on the internet. But all she'd unearthed was one paragraph explaining his family history and the fact that the Piras and Cossu banks had merged a few years ago. Cesario's personal life had not been mentioned, and it was a shock to now discover that he was married. Where were his wife and son? she wondered. Why didn't they live at the castle with him?

Her arms were aching from holding Sophie. Aware that the baby would wake again soon and need a bath and feed, she tried to dismiss the enigmatic master of the Castello del Falco to the back of her mind as she laid Sophie in the cot and went to inspect the room where *she* was to sleep.

Her room was smaller than the nursery, but no less charming, with pale walls and soft green curtains and bedspread. She would love a cup of tea, Beth thought wearily. And something to eat would be good; the hollow feeling in her stomach reminded her that she hadn't eaten anything since the piece of toast she'd had before she'd left her flat in East London that morning.

She wondered if she dared pull the bell rope to summon the maid, but she felt like a fraud. She had worked as a nanny for several rich families, and although she had shared a certain amount of intimacy with her employers' lives she had never forgotten that she was a member of the household staff—and she'd certainly never had a maid wait on her before.

Maybe a shower would take her mind off her hunger pangs? And there was still that half-eaten cheese sandwich she had bought on the plane in her handbag, she remembered. She would make do with that.

The heartrending cries of a baby drifted along the corridor. Pausing at the top of the stairs, Cesario felt his mind fly back to the first months after Nicolo had been born, when he and Raffaella had taken it in turns to pace the nursery, trying to soothe their restless son.

He had once read that becoming parents for the first time often put a strain on a marriage. But the birth of their son had resulted in an unexpected closeness between him and Raffaella, he brooded. Their devotion to Nicolo had created a bond between them. But their harmonious relationship had been short-lived, and by the time of Nicolo's second birthday Raffaella had started an affair with an artist who had been employed to carry out restoration work on the Castello del Falco's antique paintings.

'You cannot blame me for falling in love with another man,' she had told Cesario when he had confronted her. 'Our marriage was a business arrangement and there has never been any love between us. I'm not sure you are even capable of loving someone. Your heart is made of the same impenetrable stone as the walls of this castle.'

'I love my son,' Cesario had replied fiercely. 'Go to your lover if that's what you want, but you will not take Nicolo. I will never give him up.'

Unable to bear the thought of being separated from Nicolo, of the little boy growing up with a stepfather, he had immediately applied to the courts for custody of his son. He had agreed that Raffaella should have access visits. Remembering how devastated he had been when his own mother had left, it had never been his desire to prevent Nicolo from seeing his mother.

But he had underestimated the power of love, Cesario thought bitterly. Raffaella had been torn between her lover and her son. Her plan to snatch Nicolo from the castle would have been successful but for the fact that Cesario had returned home from a business trip a day earlier than expected. The ensuing row had been acrimonious—a furious exchange between two people who had never loved each other but who both loved their child.

If only he had not lost his temper. If only he had tried to reach an amicable agreement with Raffaella instead of angrily threatening to stop her visiting Nicolo. Regret burned like poison in Cesario's gut.

In an attempt to calm the situation between them he had left her alone to say goodbye to Nicolo, but while he had been in his study she had bundled the little boy into her car and driven away.

The screech of tyres on the twisting, wet mountain road still haunted his dreams. The terrifying silence that had followed still tortured his soul. He had run. *Dio*, he had run as he had never run before—like a man fleeing from the devil. But he had been too late.

Cesario dragged his mind back to the present, his nostrils flaring as he drew a harsh breath and sought to bring his emotions under control. The cries were growing louder. Tonight another child was in the nursery—a child who, astoundingly, might be his.

His jaw tightened and he strode along the corridor, intent on finding out why Sophie's guardian was apparently not taking care of her.

* * *

'Come on, sweetheart, let's see if holding you over my shoulder helps,' Beth murmured as she lifted Sophie up from the change mat. The baby had been crying for nearly an hour, and although she was regularly unsettled at this time of night Beth felt a rising sense of despair. After four months of disturbed nights she was utterly exhausted. But there was no chance she could go to bed until she had managed to settle Sophie.

Patting the baby gently on the back, she wandered over to the window and looked down at the courtyard below. It was dark now, but a little while ago car headlights had blazed as the party guests had departed from the castle.

Watching them, Beth had been tempted to slip downstairs with Sophie and plead for someone to take them to Oliena. The discovery that Cesario had a wife and son had complicated an already difficult situation. Part of her felt it would be better for everyone if she disappeared from the castle and had no further contact with Cesario Piras. She would manage to bring Sophie up on her own, she assured herself. Money would be tight, but she'd get by somehow.

But would that be fair on Sophie? her conscience demanded. What right did she have to prevent the truth about the baby's parentage from being known? And if Cesario *was* her father surely it would be better for Sophie if he played a role in her life as he had stated he would want to do.

So all the guests had driven away, and now the courtyard was deserted except for the hideous stone gargoyles whose evil faces were illuminated by the moonlight. Once again the thought that she was trapped in Cesario's forbidding fortress sent a shiver through Beth. She had no reason to fear him, she reminded herself. But the image of his scarred face seemed to have been burned onto her retinas, and the memory of his hard grey eyes had a strangely un-settling effect on her.

Sophie had quietened for a few minutes when she had been picked up, but now she started to cry again and would not be pacified. Singing to her sometimes helped, and Beth was on the second verse of 'Golden Slumbers' when a deep, gravelly voice from the doorway made her spin round.

'What's wrong with her?'

For some reason Cesario seemed even taller and more commanding here in the nursery than he had downstairs in the library. Beth's eyes flew to his face and she caught her breath, her heart suddenly racing.

His sharp gaze noted her reaction and he gave a grim smile. 'It's not pretty, is it?' he said, touching his scar. 'I apologise if you find my appearance disturbing.'

'I don't—of course I don't.' Colour flared on her cheeks. She was mortified that he thought she had been staring at him. The truth was she *did* find him disturbing, she ac-knowledged ruefully, but not in the way he meant. She could not seem to prevent her eyes from focusing on his mouth, and once again she imagined him slanting his lips over hers and kissing her with the kind of searing passion she had read about in books but never experienced per-sonally.

'Nothing is *wrong* with Sophie, exactly,' she explained hurriedly. 'She's always unsettled at this time of night. The health visitor said that lots of babies suffer from colic in the first few months, and that she'll grow out of it. But I hate seeing her like this,' she admitted as she cradled the inconsolable baby in her arms. 'I wish I could help her. I've tried walking up and down and rocking her but noth-ing's working tonight.'

There was no hint of impatience in Beth's voice even though she was clearly dead on her feet from tiredness, Cesario noted. She looked even paler than when she had first arrived at the castle, and the purple shadows beneath her eyes added to her air of fragility.

She had changed out of her shabby clothes into an equally shabby dressing gown, which had probably once been pale pink but through age and washing was now an unbecoming shade of sludge. The belt tied tightly around her waist emphasised her extreme slenderness. She looked as though she would snap in half in a strong wind, Cesario thought impatiently. She was not the type of woman he was usually attracted to, yet something about her kept drawing his gaze back to her face.

Her skin was bare of make-up and as smooth as porcelain, and her almond-shaped green eyes were captivating. There was an intriguing air of innocence about her, he mused, and although when he had first seen her he had dismissed her as ordinary-looking he saw now that she possessed an unassuming beauty that he found beguiling.

Frowning at the unexpected train of his thoughts, he crossed the nursery and stared down at Sophie, whose cries were reaching a crescendo. 'Perhaps she's hungry?'

'I tried to give her the rest of her bottle a few minutes ago but she refused it. More likely she's full of wind. I think she gulps in air when she feeds during the day, and that makes her feel uncomfortable,' Beth said, unable to disguise the weariness in her voice.

'Let me take her.'

Startled by the unexpected request, Beth instinctively tightened her hold on the baby. She had looked after Sophie on her own since she had brought her home from the hospital six weeks after her premature birth, and she felt reluctant to hand her over to a stranger. But if it was proved that Cesario was Sophie's father he would have a legal and moral right to help care for his child, she reminded herself.

'She might get upset if she's held by someone she's not used to,' she mumbled.

'I doubt she'll be any more upset than she already is,' Cesario said dryly, as Sophie's high-pitched cries intensified.

Beth hesitated a moment longer, and then held out the screaming infant to him.

Cesario tensed, a host of emotions swirling inside him. He suddenly regretted asking to hold Sophie. He did not know if she was his child, so why get involved? he asked himself. But the baby's cries had triggered an instinctive response deep within him to comfort her just as he had once comforted his son.

Panic gripped him. He did not want to be reminded of Nicolo. The memories hurt too much. But Beth was staring at him, clearly confused because he had not taken Sophie from her. Fighting a strong urge to turn away and stride out of the nursery, he stretched out his arms and lifted the baby against his chest.

She was so tiny, and she weighed next to nothing. Something fierce, almost primitive, unfurled inside him as he acknowledged how incredibly vulnerable she was.

Could she really be his daughter?

He bent his head and rested his cheek on Sophie's silky-soft dark hair. Her evocatively sweet scent—a mixture of milk and baby powder—reminded him painfully of Nicolo. But as he gently rocked Sophie and her cries subsided a sensation of peace swept over him. Another child could never replace the son he had lost, but if Sophie was his maybe his life would have meaning once more rather than being simply an existence.

'Don't cry, *piccola*,' he murmured softly.

Perhaps it was the deep timbre of his voice, or the rumble from his chest as he spoke that captured Sophie's attention. Gradually her cries lessened and she hiccupped, lifting her head to focus on him with huge, unblinking brown eyes. For several seconds she regarded him solemnly, tears still glistening on her long lashes. And then, to Cesario's amazement, her little rosebud mouth curved into a smile.

Dio mio! He caught his breath. She was so beautiful. He felt a curious sensation, as though a hand was squeezing his heart. First thing tomorrow he would arrange a DNA test, and if it was proved that Sophie was his daughter he would welcome her into his life, he vowed silently.

Beth watched in disbelief as Sophie snuggled into Cesario's neck and made the little snuffling noise that she always did when she was dropping off to sleep. The silence was bliss after the baby's piercing screams.

It was stupid to feel jealous because Cesario had managed to soothe Sophie where she had failed, she told herself. But she could not keep the stiffness from her voice as she commented, 'You must have a magic touch. I've been trying to settle her for more than an hour.'

'If she had been crying for that long she was probably worn out.' His gaze still locked on the child in his arms, Cesario walked over to the cot and laid her in it before tucking the blankets around her.

Beth was taken aback by his gentleness. She hadn't expected this big, stern-faced man to behave with such tenderness as he had shown to Sophie. But before she had arrived at the Castello del Falco she had been unaware that he already had a child.

She ran her fingers over the polished wooden end-panel of the cot, which was decorated with exquisitely carved rabbits and squirrels, and recalled the second-hand cot she had bought for Sophie. It hadn't looked too bad once she had repainted it, she thought ruefully. But it was nothing compared to this beautiful antique.

'Thank you for allowing Sophie to sleep here. This cot is amazing. Is it very old?'

'It was commissioned by one of my ancestors in the early seventeen hundreds. Documents in the library show that the then master of the Castello del Falco and his wife had been childless for twenty years before she became pregnant and gave birth to a son,' Cesario explained, keeping his voice low, so as not to wake Sophie. 'I imagine that my ancestor was overjoyed to finally have an heir, and he requested the most skilled craftsmen to make furniture for his son's nursery.'

'The butler told me that this used to be *your* son's room.' Beth hesitated when she saw Cesario stiffen but could not contain her curiosity. 'Teodoro said that he no longer lives at the castle?'

'No.'

From his curt response it was clear that Cesario did not wish to continue with the subject. His face was shuttered, and the sudden bleakness in his eyes made Beth wish she had kept quiet. Whatever mystery surrounded his son, it was no business of hers.

But after a moment, to her surprise, he continued harshly. 'Nicolo and his mother died in an accident four years ago. He was just two years old.'

'I'm sorry.' She was stunned by his shocking revelation,

and her response sounded banal and inadequate, but she did not know what else to say. Nothing about Cesario Piras was as she had expected. The impression she had gained from Mel was that he was a womanizer who had not even bothered to ask her name before he'd had sex with her.

Of course Mel had been used to that kind of boorish behaviour from men, she thought heavily. They had never discussed it, but she wasn't completely naive. She had guessed that Mel had occasionally supplemented her income from her job as a glamour model by offering a more intimate service to men she met at parties.

The idea that Cesario might have paid to sleep with Mel had made Beth reluctant to search for him. She had been convinced that he would not be interested in a baby who had resulted from a cold-blooded sexual encounter, and the only reason she had come to Sardinia was because she had promised Mel.

But Cesario did not act like a heartless playboy. He was a widower who had lost his wife and son in tragic circumstances. And, although it was not yet known if Sophie was his child, his gentleness when he had cradled her in his arms had brought a lump to Beth's throat and evoked a wistful longing that her own father had cared about her enough to stick around during her childhood.

She stared down at Sophie's angelic little face. 'I can't imagine how terrible it must be to lose a child. I may not have given birth to Sophie but I love her as much as if she was my own baby. I couldn't bear it if anything happened to her. She's all I have left of Mel,' she said huskily. 'Since I was twelve years old Mel was the only person I cared about and who cared about me.'

She blinked away her tears and lifted her head to meet Cesario's hooded gaze. 'What will happen if the DNA test reveals that you are Sophie's father?' she asked desperately. 'You said that you will want her to live here at the castle. But I have been a mother to her since the day she was born and she needs me. You can't send me away from her. It would be too cruel.'

The glimmer of tears in Beth's vivid green eyes had an unsettling effect on Cesario. He knew nothing about her other than what she had told him, and until he'd heard back from the private investigator he'd called an hour ago to check her out he had no reason to trust her or believe her story. But her emotive outburst had struck a chord in him.

'Nothing can be decided until the results of the test are known,' he said tersely. He moved away from the cot. 'For now, I suggest you get to bed. Will Sophie sleep for the rest of the night?'

'She'll probably wake at about three for a feed. Because she's so tiny she still needs a bottle during the night,' Beth explained. 'But then she usually sleeps soundly for six or seven hours.' She could not hold back a yawn. 'Actually, her sleep pattern works well for me because in England I start work at 5:00 a.m and finish at nine every morning. I leave Sophie with my neighbour.'

Cesario frowned. 'What work do you do that early in the day?'

'I clean offices for a big company close to where I live. My neighbour Maureen's husband is a postman. She's used to getting up early when he goes to work, and she babysits until I get home from my shift.'

'You work as a cleaner?'

Something in his tone made Beth flush. 'It's not easy to find a job which fits in with caring for a baby,' she said defensively. She was usually mild-natured, so perhaps it was because she was tired but his disdainful expression sent a spurt of anger through her. 'There's nothing wrong with being a cleaner. It's a vital service. You must employ dozens of domestic staff to look after this huge castle—it's not done by magic, you know.'

Cesario's dark brows winged upwards. So the little brown mouse had a temper. Twin spots of colour briefly flared on Beth's cheeks, but they faded, leaving her looking deathly pale. His mouth tightened.

'I was not expressing a criticism of your job—merely thinking that it is no wonder you resemble a wraith when you clearly get little sleep. And from the look of you—' his eyes skimmed over her slender figure '—not enough time to eat regular meals.'

Beneath his scrutiny Beth was conscious that her faded old dressing gown was fit for the bin. Looking down, she realised that the front was gaping open and she quickly drew the edges together. Not that her body was very exciting, she acknowledged ruefully. Cesario looked distinctly unimpressed by her lack of curves. She guessed he favoured voluptuous blondes. Presumably it had been Mel's provocative sex-appeal that had attracted Cesario to sleep with her a year ago.

For some reason the thought evoked a corrosive burning sensation in the pit of Beth's stomach. How on earth could she feel jealous of her best friend who was no longer alive? she asked herself disgustedly.

It suddenly seemed to have been a very long day and she was desperate to be alone. 'I do eat,' she told him curtly. 'But I'm naturally scrawny. I admit I'm very tired, though, so I'll say goodnight, Mr Piras.'

Scrawny was not the word he would have used to describe Beth Granger, Cesario brooded. He could not understand why her fragile figure and elfin features were having such a profound effect on him, but the stirring of sexual desire in his groin was as insistent as it was unexpected.

Irritated with himself, he strode towards the door. 'My name is Cesario,' he reminded her. '*Buonanotte*, Beth. I hope you and Sophie both sleep well.'

CHAPTER FOUR

AFTER checking on Sophie, Beth went straight to bed. She resolutely pushed all thoughts of Cesario to the back of her mind and fell asleep almost instantly.

A strange rumbling noise dragged her from a disturbing dream where she had been running down a long corridor lined with evil-looking stone gargoyles which turned into living creatures. She sat up, her heart racing, and switched on her bedside lamp.

Her watch showed that it was 2:00 a.m. The castle was silent, and she wondered if the noise had been part of her dream. But then it came again, as loud and violent as thunder. The storm must have moved closer. But she had never known thunder to growl continuously for so long. Going back to sleep was impossible when the noise was so loud.

Another booming crash seemed to make the walls of the castle shake. She leapt out of bed and hurried through to the nursery. Sophie was still sleeping peacefully and Beth was loath to disturb her. It seemed safer to leave the baby in the sturdy wooden cot while she went to investigate what was happening.

The corridor outside the nursery was illuminated by wall lamps which cast long shadows and flickered over several portraits housed in ornate frames. The haughty-looking men and women must be Cesario's ancestors, she guessed. Their black eyes seemed to follow her, and she could not repress a little shiver as she walked towards the head of the stairs.

There were no signs of life. Cesario and his staff must all be in bed. A terrible noise, louder than anything that had gone before, resounded through the castle. Panic-stricken, she screamed, and at that moment a door on the other side of the landing flew open.

'What's happened?' a gravelly voice demanded.

Cesario stood in the doorway, his big broad-shouldered frame silhouetted in the light that streamed from the room behind him. He must have been in bed and on hearing the noise had dragged on his trousers. But his chest was bare, and in spite of her terror Beth felt a little tremor of something that was definitely not fear run down her spine.

He was devastatingly sexy, with a toned, muscular physique that made her feel weak at the knees. Darkly tanned skin gleamed like burnished copper in the lamplight. His black tousled hair brushed his shoulders and his chest was covered with a mass of wiry hairs that arrowed down over his abdomen.

'Are you hurt?'

Suddenly conscious that she was staring at him, Beth hastily dropped her gaze.

'No. I…I was scared. That noise—what is it?'

'I don't know.' He walked towards her, frowning when another thunderous crash rent the air.

'At first I thought it was the storm, but it sounds as though the mountain is falling down,' Beth said shakily. 'Should we leave the castle?'

'Definitely not. The Castello del Falco has stood for seven hundred years and we're safer here than anywhere.'

Cesario looked grim. 'You may be right about the mountain, though. The heavy rain that has been falling for the past few days could have triggered a landslide.'

Beth gasped. 'But if part of the mountain is falling surely the castle will fall too?' Her heart was racing so fast that she found it hard to breathe, but her mind was focused on one thing. 'I left Sophie in the nursery. I must go and get her.'

She spun round, intent on racing back to the nursery, but a wave of dizziness like the one she had experienced when she had climbed the stairs earlier swept over her. The walls of the corridor seemed to be closing in on her, and she cried out as she fell forwards into black nothingness.

Growling an oath, Cesario lunged towards Beth and caught her as she crumpled. No wonder she had fainted, he thought as he lifted her in his arms and strode into his bedroom. She weighed next to nothing. He glanced down at her and his mouth tightened as he studied her hollow cheeks and the prominent line of her collarbone. What *was* it with women and dieting? He had never found extreme thinness attractive, which made his reaction to Beth all the more surprising.

She was not his type—so why had a flood of heat surged through him the instant he had swept her into his arms? And why did the brush of her silky brown hair against his bare chest evoke a throb of fierce, primitive lust in his groin? It did not help that her cotton nightgown was so thin he could see the outline of her body through it. The strap had slipped off her shoulder, exposing the upper slope of one small, pale breast, and the darker skin of her nipple was clearly visible through the material.

Her eyelashes fluttered against her white cheeks and then slowly lifted. Huge green eyes focused on him and

Cesario felt uncomfortable that he had been looking at her without her knowledge. He felt like a voyeur, and quickly lowered her onto the bed and swung away.

'Sophie!' Struggling against the blackness that was threatening to suck her back down, and the horrible sensation that she was going to be sick, Beth hung on to the one thing that mattered. Feeling disorientated, she let her eyes scan an unfamiliar room—a vast room, with dark wood-panelled walls and an enormous fireplace. The four-poster bed she was lying on was ornately carved and draped with swathes of rich burgundy silk.

She remembered the strange, terrifying noises and Cesario's warning of a possible landslide. If anything happened to Sophie…

She swung her legs over the side of the bed and gasped when a firm hand gripped her shoulder.

'Let me go. I want to go back to the nursery.'

'I've just been to check on Sophie and she's still fast asleep. Here—drink this.'

A glass was thrust into Beth's hand. With Cesario looming over her she had little option but to take a sip of the amber liquid and she choked as fiery heat burned the back of her throat.

'What is it?' she croaked when she could speak.

'Brandy. You fainted,' Cesario told her tersely. 'Drink it. It might put some colour back in your face.'

He was so forceful that she did not have the nerve to argue. She took another tiny sip, wrinkling nose in disgust. 'I never drink spirits.'

'Or eat food, from the look of you. I can only assume you are the type of woman who is obsessed with her looks and determined to diet until you resemble a skeleton.'

His derisive comment did what the brandy had failed

to do and caused angry colour to flare in her cheeks. 'I told you—I'm naturally thin. I do eat.' But admittedly not very well, Beth acknowledged silently, thinking of the days when looking after Sophie took up so much of her time that all she could be bothered to cook for herself was toast.

'Then why did you pass out?'

She sighed, wishing Cesario would let the matter drop. 'I'm probably still a bit anaemic. I saw a doctor a couple of months ago because I kept feeling dizzy, and a blood test confirmed that my red blood cell count was low. He suggested that I take iron tablets and a vitamin supplement.'

'And did you take them?'

'I took the ones the doctor gave me, but I couldn't afford to buy any more.' She flushed when he gave her an impatient look. 'Why are you so interested in the state of my health?'

How could he explain that Beth's fragile appearance aroused his protective instincts? Cesario did not understand why she triggered such deeply primitive urges inside him. Lust, yes, but also an inexplicable desire to take care of her.

The usual women he met at parties and business functions were brittle socialites who were perfectly capable of looking out for themselves. And there was no reason to suppose that this woman was any different, he reminded himself.

'Surely you must realise it is important to take care of your health for Sophie's sake? You insist that you are devoted to her, but what would happen to her if you became seriously ill? If it is proved that she is my child how could you think I would allow you to take her back to England when you plainly cannot look after yourself properly, let alone a baby.' His eyes narrowed. 'But perhaps you were expecting me to hand over a big maintenance settlement so that you could pay for childcare and not have to be bothered with her yourself?'

'I didn't expect *anything* from someone who thinks it's okay to have unprotected sex with a stranger,' Beth retaliated. It was so out of character for her to lose her temper, but Cesario's arrogance and his implication that she regarded Sophie as a means to getting her hands on his fortune goaded her beyond endurance. 'If you want my opinion, I think you're despicable,' she told him, her voice shaking with emotion. 'You must have known there was a risk Mel could fall pregnant. I suppose that's why you had already disappeared from the hotel room when she woke up in the morning? You didn't want to take responsibility for the possible outcome of your night of fun and so you didn't stick around long enough to find out her name or give her details of how to contact you if she needed to.'

Cesario's jaw hardened at her accusations, but to his shame he could not refute them. 'I've explained that I have no memory of that night.'

'That doesn't excuse what you did.'

'Or didn't do,' he said tightly. 'Until the results of a DNA test are known we only have your friend's word that I was the man she slept with.'

'Mel was absolutely certain when she saw your picture in the newspaper that you are Sophie's father.'

Beth felt intimidated by Cesario as he towered over her. She slid off the bed, but still had to tilt her head to look at him. She studied him covertly from beneath her lashes and felt a peculiar coiling sensation in the pit of her stomach as her eyes roamed over his naked chest. Seconds ago she had been furious with him, but now it was not anger that was making her heart beat uncomfortably fast.

His body had the sculpted perfection of a work of art, with the powerful muscles of his chest and abdomen clearly delineated beneath his satiny golden skin. Beth had never touched a man's unclothed torso before, and she was shocked by her urgent longing to skim her hands over Cesario's rippling muscles and follow the path of dark hairs that disappeared beneath the waistband of his trousers.

He was a callous womaniser, she reminded herself. Either he was lying when he said he did not remember the night he had spent with Mel, or he really had been so drunk that his mind was blank. Neither scenario earned respect. He was not the sort of man she could ever have imagined she would be attracted to, but it seemed that the mysterious alchemy of sexual desire paid no heed to the things she believed were important. Respect and admiration counted for nothing, she discovered, compared with the fierce yearning she felt for him to crush her against his bare chest and plunder her mouth with hungry passion.

The silence in the room was so intense that Beth was conscious of each breath she took. Part of her brain registered that the crashing noise from outside had stopped. She should return to her room and try to sleep before Sophie woke for her next feed, but she seemed to be trapped by invisible bonds and she could not prevent her eyes from straying to Cesario's face.

Her heart gave a jolt when she discovered him staring at her with a burning intensity that sent molten heat coursing through her veins. Slowly and deliberately he trailed his gaze over her. Glancing down, Beth was embarrassed to realise that her nightdress was so thin from age and frequent washing that he could probably see right through it.

If only she had pulled on her dressing gown before she had rushed out of the nursery. Her breasts felt heavy, and to her horror she saw that her nipples had hardened and were jutting against the almost sheer fabric of her nightdress. Mortified by her body's betrayal, and confused by the reaction to him that she seemed powerless to control, she stared rigidly at the carpet, sure that he would make a mocking comment.

He exhaled heavily, as if, like hers, his breath had been trapped in his lungs. A hand cupped her chin and forced her head up, and a tremor ran through Beth when she saw the hard glitter in his steel-grey eyes.

'I would not have forgotten if *you* had shared my bed,' he said harshly.

She flushed, recalling that he had made the same statement when she had first spoken to him in the castle's great hall. The disparaging look he had given her then had revealed what he thought of her.

'I'm quite aware that I am plain,' she told him, her voice stiff with hurt pride.

He gave a rough laugh, as if he was surprised by her words. 'You cannot believe that.' Almost as if he could not help himself, he traced the delicate line of her jaw with his fingertips, his touch as light as if she were made of fragile porcelain. *'Sei bella,'* he said huskily. 'I find you very lovely, Beth Granger.'

His face was so close to hers that she could feel his warm breath whisper across her lips. Time, her heartbeat—both seemed to be suspended. Was he going to kiss her? Did she want him to?

Dear heaven, he was a sorcerer and she was falling under his spell, Beth thought wildly. Was this how he had seduced Mel? Had he murmured sweet lies in his gravelly, sexy accent and mesmerised her with the sultry gleam in his eyes that promised untold delights?

Luckily the sound of her name restored her sanity. Boring, insipid Beth Granger was certainly *not* beautiful, she thought dully. If she was, she might have been fostered as a child instead of spending all her teenage years in care. She bit her lip as memories surfaced of having her photograph taken at the children's home. Photos of the kids in care had been kept with their files and shown to prospective foster families, but it had seemed that only the pretty girls got picked.

Mel had been fostered a few times, but none of her foster parents had been able to cope with her challenging behaviour and after a few months she'd been sent back to the care home. Like an unwanted Christmas present, she'd joked. But at least Mel had been given the chance to be part of a family, Beth thought. It had been a salutary lesson to realise that she was being judged by her appearance—and found wanting.

She had reached adulthood firmly believing that she was unattractive. It was just another of life's disappointments, she'd told herself. Her best attribute was her common sense. But she was ashamed to admit that for a few breathless moments she had been fooled by the look of desire in Cesario's eyes. A handsome playboy like him was not going to be interested in an unremarkable office cleaner like her, her prosaic mind pointed out.

But maybe he did not care what she looked like. Maybe he just wanted sex with any woman he believed was available—like he had with Mel. Feeling sick at the idea that he might think she was an easy lay, she jerked away from him and folded her arms across her chest to hide her body's shameful response to his potent masculinity.

'There is no chance of me ever sharing your bed, so you won't have to worry about your memory lapses,' she informed him, with an icy dignity that was somewhat spoiled by the tremor in her voice. 'I think you should concentrate on trying to remember the night you spent with Mel—the night I believe your daughter was conceived.'

His eyes gleamed dangerously. She sensed she had angered him, and steeled herself for his caustic retaliation, but the simmering silence was broken by the sound of a baby's cries.

Her brow wrinkled. 'How can I hear Sophie when she is in the nursery?'

'I switched on the baby monitor.' Cesario nodded towards the device plugged into a wall socket. 'I always used it when Nicolo was...here.' He had been about to say *alive*, but the stark reminder that his son was no longer alive caused a shaft of pain inside him. 'I knew you were tired and I thought if you were deeply asleep you might not hear Sophie if she stirred.'

'I always hear her, so you needn't worry.'

Beth stared at Cesario and caught her lower lip with her teeth. She did not know what to make of him. His concern for Sophie was unexpected, and did not fit in with the man she had supposed him to be. A few hours ago he had been unaware that he might have fathered a daughter. But, far from rejecting Sophie, he had made it clear that if she was his child he would take responsibility for her.

But what about *her*? Beth wondered fearfully. What place would she have in Sophie's life if Cesario decided he wanted the baby to live here at his castle? She wished now that she had not come to Sardinia—wished that she had kept Sophie's existence a secret. But it was too late for regrets. A DNA test would determine the truth, and if necessary she would fight for her right to be Sophie's mother—as Mel had wanted.

Another wail from the baby monitor jerked Beth into action. 'I must go to her,' she muttered, and hurried from Cesario's room, thankful to escape his brooding gaze.

What in hell's name was the matter with him? Cesario asked himself furiously as he stood staring through the doorway long minutes after Beth had fled from him, a fragile wraith in her wispy nightgown that did little to conceal her slender figure. Why had he come on to her like that? No wonder she had looked at him with such wariness in her wide green eyes.

But it had not been fear that had made her tremble for those few moments when he had stood so close to her that he had been aware of the erratic thud of her heart. There had been a fierce, inexplicable connection between them, and he knew she had felt it just as he had. He swore savagely. He had not desired a woman for months. So why was his body burning up for a pale, elfin woman whose reasons for seeking him out were highly suspect?

First thing in the morning he would arrange for the DNA test to be done and determine if the baby that Beth had brought to the castle was his, he decided as he strode into his *en-suite* bathroom and set the shower setting to cold in the hope of cooling his heated flesh. He did not share Beth's conviction that he had slept with her friend—it seemed unlikely that he had retained no memory of having sex with Melanie Stewart, however drunk he had been.

There was a good chance Sophie was not his child. If that was the case he would ensure that Beth Granger and her tiny charge were on the first flight back to England, and he would no longer be disturbed by the slanting green eyes that he was convinced had cast a spell over him.

He frowned as he recalled how she had told him she worked an early-morning shift as a cleaner and left Sophie with a neighbour. It was obvious from her shabby clothes that she had little money. His thoughts turned to the beautiful baby girl in the nursery and something tugged on his insides as he remembered Sophie's gummy smile. If she was not his child perhaps he would make a financial arrangement so that Beth could give up her job and concentrate on caring for the baby, he brooded. After all, he had more money than he knew what to do with, and losing Nicolo had made him realise that he cared nothing for the things that had once been important to him, such as wealth and power. Everything seemed meaningless—including his own life.

The hands on Beth's watch showed that it was nine o'clock, and the stream of light filtering through the gap in the curtains indicated that it was morning—which meant that she had overslept and missed her cleaning shift. Horrified, she threw back the sheets—and then took a steadying breath as her brain caught up. She had spent the night at Cesario Piras's castle, and without her alarm clock to wake her at four-thirty, as it did every other morning, she had slept embarrassingly late.

Sophie had settled straight after her 3:00 a.m. feed, and now, when Beth stole into the nursery, she found the baby still sleeping peacefully. As she moved away from the cot there was a light knock on the door, and a moment later a woman whom she guessed was one of the castle staff entered the nursery, bearing a tray.

'Ah, you are awake and the *bambina* is still asleep—that is good. My name is Filomena,' the woman introduced herself in a loud whisper. 'I am cook for Signor Piras and I look after his castle. All the other staff—they do what I tell them.'

Beth could well believe it. Filomena was short in stature, and cosily plump, but her flashing black eyes warned of a fiery and formidable personality. However, her smile was welcoming, and when she peeped at Sophie her face softened.

'Angioletto,' she breathed before she set the tray down on the table by the window. 'You can eat breakfast while the *bambina* sleeps,' she told Beth. 'If she wakes I will hold her while you finish.'

The aroma of coffee and freshly baked rolls made Beth's stomach rumble appreciatively, and the bowl of peaches and cherries looked as inviting as the dish beside it containing creamy yoghurt. But if Sophie acted true to form she would undoubtedly stir the minute Beth started eating, she thought ruefully.

She smiled shyly at Cesario's cook. 'That's very kind of you, but I'm sure you must be busy…'

Beady black eyes fixed her with a stern look. 'Signor Piras say to Filomena that you must eat—so you eat.' She gave Beth a cursory inspection and sniffed. 'You are too thin. You will never find a husband.'

Beth did not explain that following her father's devastating betrayal of her mother she had decided she never wanted a husband. Instead, she deemed it wiser to subside into a chair and help herself to a roll. 'Is Signor Piras's word law?' she murmured.

'Of course,' Filomena said cheerfully. 'He is the master of the Castello del Falco. He is *il capo*. How you say? The boss.'

'Yes, I imagine he is,' Beth said dryly, recalling his hard features and granite-grey eyes. Cesario was king of his castle, and his position as head of one of Italy's biggest banks must mean that he was immensely powerful.

But she had witnessed a gentler side to his nature when he had rocked Sophie off to sleep and could not help but be intrigued by him.

Her mind lingered on those few heart-stopping moments in his room when she had thought that he was going to kiss her, and a little tremor ran through her. Of course she hadn't wanted him to. Not a man like him—a man who slept around and was careless of the consequences. She stared at the tray in front of her. He was also a man who had instructed his cook to bring her breakfast. He was probably just being a polite host, she told herself firmly, he was not interested in her welfare.

The torrential rain of the previous night had eased to a fine drizzle which continued to fall from the leaden sky. Beth had spent the morning in the nursery with Sophie, but now, after lunch—which Filomena had brought, and then watched her like a hawk while she ate—a glimmer of sunshine broke through the clouds outside the window.

'We'll go for a walk,' she told the baby as she dressed her in an all-in-one suit. At home she tried to take Sophie out in the fresh air most days. The one-bedroom flat she rented in a grim tower block in East London was cramped, especially now that it was filled with baby paraphernalia, but luckily the Hackney Marshes were close by, and provided an oasis of green in a busy part of London.

Teodoro carried the baby buggy down the castle steps, and once Beth had strapped Sophie into it and tucked a blanket round her she strolled around the courtyard. The Castello del Falco was much less forbidding in daylight, she noted. Built on a plateau close to the summit of the mountain, it was surrounded by higher mountains which rose towards the sky, their lower slopes covered in dense woodland and their grey peaks resembling jagged teeth.

The castle was like something from a fairy tale, Beth mused. Even the stone gargoyles looked impish and mischievous in the sunlight, rather than wickedly cruel as they had when she had arrived during the storm last night. Lulled by the motion of the pushchair, Sophie had drifted off to sleep. There seemed no point in disturbing her by carrying her back inside, so Beth explored the well-tended gardens at the rear of the castle, arranged in a series of terraces. Each tier was beautifully formal, with clipped yew hedges bordered by gravel pathways, ornamental fountains splashing into pools, and graceful marble statues standing serenely amid the lush greenery.

It would be an amazing place for a child to grow up. Beth gave a rueful sigh as she recalled the graffiti-strewn stairways, which were the haunt of local drug dealers, and the acres of concrete on the estate where she lived. How much better it would be for Sophie if she was Cesario's daughter and the castle became her home. But where would *she* live? she wondered fretfully. Would it be possible for her to move to the nearby town of Oliena and find some sort of job so that she could still be a part of Sophie's life?

Lost in her thoughts, she followed the path round to the front of the castle—and halted when she saw Cesario on horseback, riding into the courtyard. He was an imposing sight, and she felt her heart jolt beneath her ribs. Sitting astride a huge, powerful-looking horse, he was dressed almost entirely in black: black boots, jeans, and a leather jerkin worn over a dark grey loosely woven shirt. Curiously, on one hand he wore a thick leather glove that reached almost to his elbow. His dark hair was windswept around his hard-boned face, and even from a distance the livid scar on his cheek was clearly visible. But it did not detract from his rugged good-looks.

There was a tough, untamed quality about him that touched something deep inside Beth. He was the man of her fantasies: a pirate, an adventurer, undoubtedly a dangerous adversary and a passionate lover. She drew a ragged breath, shocked by the train of her thoughts. He was out of her league, she reminded herself. But that knowledge did not stop her traitorous body from reacting to his potent virility.

As her eyes met his glinting grey gaze she felt lightheaded, and she knew she could not blame her sudden breathlessness on her low red blood-cell count.

He walked his great black horse forward, and as he did so a shadow swooped over Beth's head. Startled by the beating sound, and the sudden rush of air that moved her hair, she glanced up to see a bird of prey circle the courtyard and land on Cesario's gloved arm.

His stern features lightened a fraction when he noticed her stunned expression. 'This is Gratia,' he told her, in the deep, gravelly voice that brought her skin out in goosebumps. 'You are honoured. Often she will not come to the glove if a stranger is near.'

'She's beautiful. What kind of bird is she?'

'A peregrine falcon—the fastest of all birds of prey. *Grazia* means grace, and she is not just swift and powerful in the air but incredibly graceful.' Cesario gave a low laugh. 'To be honest, she is the only female I have ever truly loved.'

Beth eyed the big grey and white speckled bird with its hooked beak and vicious-looking talons and wondered if he was joking. 'But…surely you loved your wife?' she faltered.

His gaze became hooded. 'If I had perhaps I would still have my son,' he said harshly.

'What do you mean?'

He shook his head. 'Forget it—it doesn't matter. I have other news that will be of far more interest to you. As I suspected, the noises we heard last night were caused by a landslide farther down the mountain.'

Recalling recent news reports of the devastating mud-slides in India caused by the monsoon, Beth gave him a worried look. 'Was anyone hurt?'

'Fortunately there are no houses on that part of the mountain. But it is a significant slide, and the road to Oliena is blocked—which means that we are temporarily cut off. We cannot get down to the town and no one can reach us here—including the doctor who I arranged to carry out the DNA test.'

She stared at him as the implication of his words sank in. 'So what can we do?'

He shrugged. 'We can't do anything except wait for the road to be cleared. And that could be several days at least.' He anticipated her next question. 'I rode out to take a look. Heavy machinery will have to be brought in to move the boulders.'

'But if the test can't be done for days, and it takes time for the results to come back, I could be stuck here for weeks.' The boss of the cleaning company where she worked would not keep her job open indefinitely, Beth thought worriedly.

Cesario glanced around the sunlit courtyard, and then up to the mountains which encircled the castle. 'I can think of worse places to be stuck,' he drawled. 'Look at it this way—our enforced captivity will give us the chance to get to know one another better, which could be important if it turns out that Sophie is my child.'

His words evoked a flare of fierce excitement in Beth that her sensible nature quickly quashed. Cesario's only interest in her was because of her role as Sophie's guardian. She would be a fool to allow her fascination with him to continue. But her heartbeat quickened when he glanced down at her and his mouth curved into a slow, sensual smile.

'Dinner will be at eight o'clock tonight. I look forward to your company, Beth,' he murmured, before he urged his horse on and rode out of the courtyard.

CHAPTER FIVE

BETH only owned one dress, and like most of her clothes she had bought it from a charity shop. Unlike the rest of her uninspiring wardrobe, however, the deep green evening dress was an exquisite creation from a well-known fashion house. Deceptively simple, with a sweetheart neckline, narrow shoulder straps and a floaty layer of chiffon over the silk underskirt, it was a testament to superb tailoring.

'I can't believe you paid next to nothing for a couture gown,' Mel had complained. 'Have you any idea how much that dress would have cost to buy new?'

Having never visited a designer boutique, Beth had only been able to guess. Haute couture was way beyond her means, and she had wondered how Mel could afford expensive clothes.

'Sometimes men like to buy me presents,' Mel had explained vaguely. 'We both know it's a tough world, and I'm not going to refuse if some guy wants to spend his money on me.'

Memories of her closest friend brought tears to Beth's eyes. The years of abuse Mel had suffered as a child had given her a hard edge, and only Beth had understood that Mel's brittle outer shell had disguised the scared little girl who still lived inside her.

'We don't need stupid foster parents,' Mel had declared. 'We're as close as sisters and we don't need anyone else.'

Now Mel was gone, and her dying wish had been for Beth to be a mother to her baby daughter. 'Love Sophie for me,' she had whispered with her last breath. Beth had given her word. It was a promise she had vowed to keep for ever, and if a DNA test proved that Cesario was Sophie's father she was determined to convince him that he must play a role in the baby's life.

Her stomach dipped at the prospect of having dinner with him as an image of him as she had seen him in the courtyard filled her mind. Even with that cruel scar he was the most devastatingly sexy man she had ever met. He exuded an air of strength and power, and when he had smiled at her she had felt again that strange sensation as if an arrow had pierced her heart.

She must *not* let her imagination run away with her, she told her reflection firmly. But she could do nothing about the glitter of excitement in her eyes or the flush of pink on her usually pale cheeks, and her hand shook a little as she applied a coat of tinted gloss to her lips. Her just-washed hair was too silky to wear up so she left it loose, wishing that she had luscious curls rather than her sleek, dead straight style.

The only piece of jewellery she possessed was a gold locket containing a photo of her mother. Flat ballerina pumps that she had dyed the same shade as her dress completed her outfit. With a final glance in the mirror she walked through the door from her room into the nursery and smiled at the maid, Carlotta, who was to watch over Sophie for the evening.

Assured that the baby was fast asleep, and that Carlotta would call her if she woke, Beth stepped into the corri-

dor and discovered Teodoro waiting to escort her down
to the dining room. She caught his look of faint surprise
and guessed he was remembering the ghastly wool coat
she had been wearing when she had arrived at the castle
the previous night. It had not been one of her better pur-
chases from the charity shop, she thought wryly, but she
had needed a winter coat and it had been all she could afford.

Like the ballroom, the dining room was a huge, high-
ceilinged room, with dark wood-panelled walls and an
enormous, intricately carved fireplace. Patterned rugs
on the stone floor gave some much needed colour to the
rather sombre décor. A long polished oak table stretched
the length of the room and Beth estimated that thirty or
more people could be seated at it. Only two places were
set at one end of the table, however, and as she entered
the room Cesario swung round from the window where
he had been staring into the darkness outside and walked
towards her.

The simmering anger that had gripped Cesario following
the telephone call he had taken half an hour ago burned
hotly inside him as his eyes roamed over Beth. To his
disgust, he could not control the sharp tug of desire that
arrowed through him and wondered how he could have
dismissed her as unworthy of a second glance when she
had first arrived at the castle.

She was as slender as a reed in a green dress which emphasised the vivid colour of her eyes. Other than a faint
sheen of gloss on her lips her face was bare of make-up,
and he was once again struck by her air of innocence. But
he knew now that it was an illusion, he thought darkly.
For all the simplicity of her dress, he could tell that it was

couture and undoubtedly expensive. Either wages for office cleaners were higher than he had realised, he mused sardonically, or Beth had acquired the dress the same way she had helped herself to a pair of diamond earrings.

His jaw hardened, but he disguised his fury with a smile that only those who knew him well would have recognised—and feared.

'Good evening, Beth.'

His eyes lingered on her for a moment, watching the soft stain of colour flare along her delicate cheekbones, and he felt a spurt of savage triumph that she could not hide the betraying sign of her awareness of him. He had no control over the sudden quickening of his pulse, and it took all his will-power to turn his head from her and glance at his butler.

'That will be all, thank you, Teodoro. Please see that Miss Granger and I are not disturbed.'

The click of the door as Teodoro left the room sounded faintly ominous, indicating as it did that she was now alone with Cesario, Beth thought with a sudden rush of nervousness. She silently ordered herself to stop being stupid as she sat down on the chair he pulled out for her. But she had always been acutely sensitive to atmosphere, and her skin prickled as she sensed an undercurrent of tension in the room.

'What would you like to drink? Filomena has prepared a chicken dish, and I was going to serve a Sauvignon Blanc with it, but there is red wine if you prefer?'

'White is fine, thank you.' She did not want to appear gauche by asking for lemonade, and perhaps a glass of wine would help her to relax. When he handed her the drink, she offered him a shy smile, but it was not reciprocated. Instead, his eyes narrowed and glittered with an expression Beth could not define.

He raised his glass and drawled in a faintly mocking tone, 'To new acquaintances.' Taking his place opposite her at the table, he indicated the first course—a selection of cold meats, local pecorino cheese and figs. 'Please begin. And while we eat,' he murmured dulcetly, 'you can tell me more about Beth Granger.'

The curious nuance in his voice caused Beth's stomach to knot and her appetite deserted her. She forced herself to sample a piece of ham and then set down her fork. 'What would you like to know?'

'Why don't you start with your career?'

'I'm not sure that working as a cleaner could be described as a career,' she said quietly.

'Ah, but I understand you are a qualified nanny and worked until fairly recently for a family in Berkshire.'

Beth's mouth suddenly felt dry. She reached for her glass and took a sip of wine, unaware that Cesario had noticed her hand shaking slightly. 'How do you know that?'

'I had you investigated.' His brows lifted at Beth's sharp intake of breath. 'How could you think I wouldn't? You've turned up at my home with a fantastical story. It is only natural that I should want to know everything about you.'

'It isn't a fantastical story. Mel was certain you are Sophie's father.'

Cesario could not *possibly* know what had happened when she had worked for the Devingtons, Beth assured herself desperately. Alicia Devington had agreed not to involve the police in return for Beth leaving Devington Hall immediately and without the month's pay she had been owed. It had been Hugo Devington's suggestion, of course, she thought bitterly. He hadn't wanted the police called in case she told them what he had done.

But she'd had no proof. It would have been the word of a lowly nanny against that of a highly respected barrister. And after Hugo had cleverly set her up to look like a thief no one would have believed her accusation that he had attempted to sexually assault her.

The memory of Hugo Devington QC's arrogant smirk as he had peeled a five pound note from the wad of cash in his wallet and offered it to her to pay for her taxi to the station was as clear in her mind as the memory of his red face and hot breath as he had shoved his sweaty hand up her skirt.

Feeling slightly sick, she forced herself to meet Cesario's gaze. 'I have nothing to hide.'

'Really?' He paused for a heartbeat, as still and watchful as a panther preparing to spring on its doomed prey. 'I thought you would want to keep the fact that you once stole a pair of diamond earrings worth forty thousand pounds well and truly hidden.'

'I didn't.' Her denial was swift and fierce, but inside she was utterly mortified by Cesario's contemptuous expression. 'It's true there was…an incident. But the police weren't involved and the only people who knew of it were Mr and Mrs Devington and me. I don't understand how your investigator could have heard about it,' she said in a low tone.

He shrugged. 'The Devingtons employ several domestic staff, all of whom were aware of the reason for your abrupt departure from Devington Hall. People like to gossip—especially after a few drinks. My private eye learned a great deal from the Devingtons' cook when he met her in the local pub.'

'Nora doesn't know the truth about what happened. Nobody does.' Beth's voice shook. 'Except me and Mr Devington.'

'Are you saying that the Cartier earrings Hugo Devington had given to his wife as a birthday present did *not* disappear from her jewellery box, and were *not* later found hidden in a drawer in your room?' Cesario demanded relentlessly.

The blood drained from Beth's face. She wanted to defend herself, but she felt intimidated by Cesario's barely leashed aggression. She hated any sort of confrontation. Her mind flew back over the years to an incident at school, when one of the girls in her class had announced that an expensive watch had disappeared from her locker.

Stephanie Blake had been one of the pretty, popular, well-off girls, and Beth had never been included in her circle of friends. When she had found the watch on the playing field, where Stephanie must have dropped it, she'd hurried to return it. But instead of thanking her the other girl had given her a suspicious look, and later Beth had overheard her discussing the probability that she had stolen the watch in the first place.

'My father says you can't trust children in care,' Stephanie had stated to her cronies. 'Beth was probably going to sell my watch, but lost her nerve.'

At fourteen, she had been too shy and lacking in self-confidence to defend herself, Beth remembered dismally.

She darted a glance at Cesario's autocratic face that looked as though it had been carved from stone and caught her lower lip with her teeth.

'I swear I didn't take the earrings. I was shocked when they were found in my room, but…I know who put them there.'

'Then why didn't you say so at the time?'

She flinched at his sardonic tone and realised it was pointless to try and convince him of her innocence. *Because no one would have believed me*, she answered his question silently. She had been an unimportant nanny, while Hugo Devington was a member of the landed gentry whose father had a place in the House of Lords. It had been easier to leave her job rather than risk being arrested for a crime she could not prove she hadn't committed.

Beth was clearly as guilty as hell, Cesario thought furiously as he stared at her across the table and noted how she refused to meet his gaze. He did not understand why the Devingtons hadn't pressed charges. Presumably they had wanted her out of their home and away from their children as quickly as possible. An opportunistic thief was hardly a good influence for innocent young minds.

She darted him a fleeting glance, and to his fury he felt a tugging sensation in his gut when he saw the faintly pleading look in her eyes. How could he feel sorry for her? he asked himself with bitter self-contempt. Her air of vulnerability was not real, and it was highly likely that her story about him being the father of her friend's baby was something she had dreamed up in an attempt to con money out of him.

'I'm giving you one last chance to tell me the real reason why you have come here,' he said coldly. 'I don't believe the child upstairs in the nursery is mine. But *if* by some miracle Sophie *is* my daughter I will not allow you to have anything more to do with her. You say she needs a mother? With your questionable morals you are hardly an ideal role model.'

Beth felt as humiliated as she had done all those years ago, when she had overheard her classmate unfairly accusing her of stealing the watch she had found. At school she had been labelled a care home kid, unwanted, unloved, and unworthy of being trusted. Nothing had changed, she thought painfully. Cesario had set himself up as judge and jury and he would never believe her side of the story.

She scraped back her chair and stood up, trembling with pent up emotion. 'My morals are not questionable,' she said fiercely. 'I am not a thief, and I never touched Alicia Devington's wretched earrings. *I* don't think a notorious playboy who sleeps around would be a good role model for Sophie,' she went on, after snatching a ragged breath. 'You've admitted you were too drunk that night to remember if you slept with Mel. Why don't we assume that you are *not* the man she spent the night with and drop the idea of doing a DNA test? I'll take Sophie back to England and you can forget about both of us.'

'You mean you would be prepared to bring her up on your own? Without any financial pay-out?' Cesario demanded, his black brows drawing together.

'I only ever wanted a bit of money to give her the things I never had when I was a child—nice clothes, trips to the cinema, maybe the occasional holiday. I don't mean expensive foreign holidays,' Beth assured him, 'just a week at the seaside somewhere. But material things don't really matter. I love Sophie, and for a child to know it's loved is the most important thing of all.'

Dio, she sounded so convincing. Could he have misjudged her? Doubt filtered into Cesario's mind. Could the story about her stealing from her employers be untrue? Perhaps nothing more than spiteful gossip and hearsay that the investigator had reported as fact?

'For Sophie's sake we must go ahead with the test,' he said abruptly. 'Her biological mother is dead, and however much you might love her she has a right to know who her father is.'

He exhaled heavily, his temper cooling as he considered the possibility that the investigator might be wrong. It had been unfair of him to react the way he had without verifying the information he had been given, he admitted. But if he was honest with himself he was annoyed by his attraction to Beth. He didn't like the way she made him feel, and he had seized on a reason to think the worst of her.

'Sit down,' he commanded, lifting his glass and taking a long sip of wine. The only way he could form a fair opinion about Beth Granger was to get to know her better; and perhaps over dinner and a few glasses of wine she would relax and open up to him. 'I'll ring for Teodoro to serve the main course.'

His arrogance was breathtaking, Beth thought furiously. She did not often lose her temper, but she was so hurt and angry she wanted to throw something at Cesario and wipe the superior expression from his face.

'Do you really expect me to continue with dinner after you've made those awful accusations and threatened to take Sophie from me?' she said bitterly. 'Do you think I have no feelings? That because I have no money or family I am somehow a lesser person and don't deserve to be treated with consideration?'

She lifted her head and met his gaze, unaware that he had noticed the shimmer of tears in her eyes.

'I don't want to eat with you. You are not pleasant company and I'd probably choke,' she told him tightly, before she wheeled away from the table and raced from the room.

* * *

'It's stopped raining at last.' Beth sighed as she stared at the sullen sky which promised more rain to come. 'I had no idea that it rained so much in Sardinia,' she said, turning away from the window to Filomena, who had brought her lunch up to the nursery and was now clearing away the plates of hardly touched food.

'You did not like my pasta with my special recipe tomato sauce?' the cook demanded.

'It's lovely, but I'm afraid I'm not hungry today.'

Filomena gave her a sharp look, but said no more about her lack of appetite. 'Some years we have a wet spring,' she said with a shrug. 'But you will see—in a few weeks the sky will be blue all day long and the sun will be too hot for your fair skin.'

Would she still be in Sardinia when the weather improved? Beth wondered. Would the results of the DNA test be known? And if, as she suspected, they proved that Cesario was Sophie's father would she be embroiled in a battle for the right to have a role in the baby's life?

After last night's confrontation with him she had been so worried she had barely slept. Maybe Sophie had sensed her tension and that was why she had been so unsettled all morning, she thought, glancing over to the cot where the baby was finally sleeping peacefully after screaming for almost an hour.

'Leave the *bambina* with me,' Filomena suggested softly. 'Go for a walk in the gardens while the rain has stopped. It is not good to be inside all the time.'

Beth shook her head. 'I don't want to leave her in case she wakes up and wants me.'

'I can take care of her if she wakes. You think I don't know about babies?' Filomena demanded. 'I have brought up six sons.'

It wouldn't do any harm to get some fresh air, Beth conceded. Maybe a walk would help get rid of her headache. She gave the cook a faint smile. 'All right. I'll go for twenty minutes. Sophie should sleep for at least an hour.'

It was too warm for her coat, she discovered, when she stepped outside a few minutes later. A pale sun had emerged from behind the clouds, although many of the higher peaks of the mountains were still shrouded in mist. Ignoring the path that led to the gardens, she walked across the courtyard and out of the main gateway. The Castello del Falco felt brooding and oppressive today, and she was glad to escape its towering grey walls.

Turning off the road that wound down the mountain, she followed a narrow footpath that at first dropped steeply before the land levelled out into fields strewn with wild flowers and bordered by dense woodland. The countryside was ruggedly beautiful, its silence only broken by birdsong and the occasional bleat from the sheep grazing some way in the distance.

It was good to forget all her worries for a while and simply enjoy being outside. The Gennargentu Mountains seemed a world away from the busy streets of East London, and as Beth walked she lost all sense of time. A strange sound carried on the breeze made her halt. It seemed to come from somewhere in the trees—a mournful howl that sent a shiver through her. She glanced around fearfully, wondering if there were wolves in Sardinia. The howling came again. Thinking it could be a child's cry, she forgot her fear and ran towards a copse of tall pine trees—but stopped dead as a sickening sight met her eyes.

'Oh, no.' Horrified, she dropped to her knees beside a dog lying on the ground with its leg caught in a trap. Wicked-looking metal teeth were gripping the animal tightly, and Beth quickly realised that she would be unable to free the wounded creature. Her heart clenched when the dog looked at her with pain-filled brown eyes. Ignoring the fact that a wounded animal might be vicious, she patted it gently, and it gave her hand a feeble lick. 'I'll go and get help,' she choked. She hated to leave the injured animal, but it would die if it was not set free soon.

'You say Beth went out an hour ago?' Cesario questioned Filomena, raising his voice above the loud cries of the baby, whom the cook was endeavouring to comfort.

'She said she was going for a walk in the gardens, but when I sent one of the staff to look for her there was no sign of her.' Filomena shook her head as she tried to feed Sophie from a bottle, but the baby spat out the teat and screamed louder. 'I cannot imagine what has happened. Signorina Beth is devoted to the *bambina* and would not leave her for long.'

Cesario's eyes were drawn to the inconsolable infant in the cook's arms, and he felt a tug of pity when he saw tears on Sophie's flushed cheeks. 'Let me hold her,' he said, stepping forward to take the baby from Filomena.

Sophie was so small and vulnerable, and so utterly distressed, that he instinctively cuddled her against his chest and spoke to her softly. 'Hush, *piccola*. Don't cry. Are you hungry, hmm?'

At the sound of his voice Sophie's screams gradually lessened, and she stared up at Cesario with huge, trusting brown eyes.

'You were always able to comfort your son,' Filomena murmured as she handed him the bottle of formula.

A shaft of pain sliced through Cesario as he was assailed by memories of Nicolo. For a moment he wanted to hand Sophie back and run from the nursery which held so many reminders of his little boy. But when he offered Sophie the teat of the bottle she took it, and made a contented sound as she began to suck.

There was no doubt she was a sweet little thing. He still found it unbelievable that she might be his child, but if a DNA test proved that she was it would be no hardship to love her, Cesario brooded. Thoughts of the test turned his mind back to Sophie's guardian, and he frowned when he glanced to the window and saw that it was raining once more.

Once Sophie had finished her feed he handed her back to Filomena and turned to speak to the maid, Carlotta. 'Tell the groom to saddle my horse,' he instructed tersely. 'I'd better go and search for Signorina Granger.'

Beth raced back across the field, desperate to find help to rescue the injured dog. As she ran, the rain started again, feeling like sharp needles on her skin and quickly soaking through her skirt and blouse. Seeking what shelter she could from the elements, she kept close to a row of thick bushes. She became aware of a pounding noise, and at first thought it was the sound of her blood pumping in her ears as she ran. But the pounding grew louder. There was a split-second's silence, and then she screamed when a huge shape, a figure—she did not know what—soared over the bushes and missed her by mere inches.

Utterly terrified, she stumbled and fell. The grass was wet beneath her cheek and she could smell the damp earth. She heard a male voice swear savagely, and then strong hands gripped her arms and she was lifted and set roughly on her feet.

'*Santa Madre!* What in hell's name are you doing?'

Cesario glared at her furiously, his jaw rigid and his unruly hair falling into his eyes. 'Where have you been? You told Filomena you were going to walk in the gardens, but no one could find you in the castle grounds. Answer me, damn it,' he growled when Beth made no sound, simply stared at him mutely, trembling with a mixture of fright, shock and an involuntary reaction to her proximity to Cesario's big, muscular body.

Behind him she could see his great black horse calmly cropping the grass. The pounding she'd heard must have been the horse's hooves as it had galloped across the field on the other side of the bushes. If Cesario and his horse had landed on her she could have been killed, she thought weakly. A wave of dizziness swept over her and her lashes fluttered against her cheeks.

'Oh, no, you don't,' she heard him mutter. 'You're not going to faint on me again, *mia belleza*.'

Cesario could not explain the irrational fear that had swept through him when he had learned that Beth had disappeared from the castle. There was no reason to suppose she had come to any harm, he had told himself as he had mounted his horse and ridden out of the courtyard to search for her. But he'd been plagued by the image of how she had looked the previous evening: pale and shaking with emotion as she had faced him across the dining table, fiercely refuting the accusation that she had stolen from her previous employers. The memory of her trying to blink back her tears had tugged on his insides, and he had felt uncomfortable with the knowledge that he had upset her.

Now, as he stared down at her white face, relief surged through him. But when his eyes roamed over her slender body and saw the firm thrust of her breasts clearly outlined beneath her wet blouse another, far more primitive emotion thundered through his veins.

Beth sensed a subtle change in Cesario. His voice was no longer harsh with anger but rough, and laced with a seductive huskiness that sent a tremor through her. She opened her eyes and was trapped by his granite-grey gaze. She felt his warm breath on her skin and her senses quivered as she inhaled the scent of him: an intoxicating mixture of his wet leather coat, the evocatively spicy cologne he wore, and something else that was intensely male and uniquely *him*.

Her brain registered all those things in the timeless seconds that trembled between them. And then his head swooped and he covered her mouth with his own.

Starbursts of pleasure instantly exploded inside her, and without conscious thought she parted her lips beneath his. Perhaps she should have been shocked, but in truth she had imagined his kiss from the moment her eyes had locked with his in the ballroom of his castle. She felt as though she had been waiting for him all her life, that she had been born for this moment with this man, and there was no thought in her head to resist him when he plundered her lips with a hunger that touched her soul.

He was not gentle, but she hadn't expected him to be, and his fierce desire, the bold thrust of his tongue into her mouth, evoked a desperate longing for him to pull her down onto the wet earth and claim her body with every pagan demand she sensed throbbed in his blood.

The few chaste kisses she had shared when she'd been on occasional dates with other men had not prepared her for Cesario's sensual onslaught. His lips grazed hers again and again, drawing a response that she was powerless to deny.

The teeming rain pounded them, running down their faces and slicking Beth's shirt to her body. The feel of the sodden material clinging to her breasts was deliciously erotic, and she could not repress a soft moan when he ran his hands down her front and traced her taut nipples jutting through the wet cotton. Sensation arrowed through her and, driven by an instinctive need to be even closer to him, she lifted her arms and curved them around his neck.

He muttered something in Italian and crushed her to him, so that her breasts were pressed against his chest. She was conscious of his hard sinews and muscles imprinted on her softer flesh, and the solid ridge of his arousal jabbed her belly, causing molten heat to pool between her thighs.

The dark stubble shading his jaw felt abrasive against her cheek but she did not care. Nothing mattered except that he should never, ever stop kissing her. Some pagan force deep inside her told her that she belonged here in his arms. That she belonged to him. She curled her fingers into his hair and then, like a blind person wanting to imprint his image on her brain, stroked his face, exploring every angle and plane and tracing the sharp edges of his cheekbones.

Her fingertips fluttered over the raised ridge of his scar. At her touch he stiffened and tore his mouth from hers, his actions so abrupt that she was unprepared and swayed dizzily for a moment. Deprived of the warmth and strength of his body she felt bereft, and wondered with a flash of despair how she could bear the aching loneliness of her life.

He dropped his arms to his sides, allowing her to step back from him. As the reality of what had happened sank in she lifted her hand to her mouth and felt its swollen softness, staring at Cesario with stunned eyes.

'Why did you do that?' she whispered.

He gave a harsh laugh, his eyes hooded and glittering with a savage hunger. 'Why? You know why, *cara*. You feel this intense attraction as strongly as I do. Maybe you resent it, and are shocked by it—just as I am. But you cannot deny the fire that burns between us.'

She could not deny her awareness of him, but she was startled by his stark admission that he desired her. He cupped her face in his hands and she watched, her heart hammering, as he lowered his head once more. Her lips parted involuntarily in readiness for him to kiss her again, but a sudden memory forced its way into her head and with a cry she pulled away from him.

'The dog! I found a dog caught in a trap,' she explained when he stared at her uncomprehendingly. 'We have to set it free or it will die. Please…' She caught hold of his arm. 'Will you come?'

'Where?' Cesario demanded tersely, fighting the temptation to snatch her back into his arms and finish what they had started, here and now on the sodden grass. He had never felt such a primitive urgency to possess a woman, but this woman with her fey beauty and slanting green eyes had surely cast a spell on him, he thought self-derisively.

'In the woods at the edge of the field.' Feeling desperately guilty that she had forgotten about the injured dog during those moments when she had been in Cesario's arms, Beth turned and started to run. She had only gone a short distance when he came alongside her, sitting astride his horse.

'Give me your hand,' he ordered. Reaching down, he ignored her shocked gasp and lifted her up onto the saddle in front of him as easily as if she weighed nothing. 'Show me where to go.'

Beth disliked heights, and a cautious glance over the horse's head revealed that the ground was a long way down.

'You're safe. I won't let you fall.' Cesario's deep voice sounded close to her ear. And, strangely, she did feel safe with her back pressed against his chest and his arms on either side of her as he flicked the reins and urged the horse into a gallop.

CHAPTER SIX

'DO YOU think you can force the trap open with something—maybe a stick or tree branch?' Beth asked Cesario anxiously as he knelt by the injured dog.

'It should release if I step on the spring mechanism,' he told her, after studying the contraption for a few minutes. 'I imagine a shepherd has had a problem with foxes worrying his sheep and has set traps to try and protect his flock. Move away. An injured animal can behave unpredictably and the dog might turn on you.'

She looked into the dog's pained eyes. 'I don't think he'll bite me,' she said softly. As she knelt down she heard a ripping sound, and gave a rueful sigh when she saw that her skirt had snagged on a bramble. 'Oh, well—like all my clothes it only cost a few pounds from a charity shop.'

'I imagine the dress you were wearing last night cost considerably more than a few pounds,' Cesario said dryly.

'Actually, no. That dress is my best bargain find, and I was pleased that the money I paid for it went to a charity supporting multiple sclerosis sufferers, because my mother had the illness for many years and eventually lost her life to it.'

With her eyes focused on the dog, Beth did not see the intent glance Cesario gave her. He stepped on the spring and the trap jaws shot apart, releasing its victim. 'Careful,' he warned, when she immediately lifted the dog up, but the animal was clearly grateful to be free and lay quiet and utterly trusting in Beth's arms.

'Its leg is cut,' she noted worriedly, seeing blood on the dog.

'A flesh wound.' Cesario gave the animal a cursory inspection. 'Set it down and I expect it will find its way back to its owner.'

He frowned when Beth turned her almond-shaped eyes on him and gave him a look that seemed to imply he was as callous as a mass-murderer.

'I'm not going to abandon the poor creature—although I suspect its owner might have done,' she said regretfully. 'It looks half starved.'

'*It* is a he.' Cesario studied the dog's matted coat. 'And he's certainly not the most attractive dog I've ever seen.'

'Just because he isn't beautiful is no reason not to give him a home,' Beth said fiercely, thinking of all the times she had been disappointed not to have been chosen by foster parents when she had lived in the children's home. 'Please can we take him back to the castle? I'm sure Filomena will allow him to stay in the kitchens—at least until his leg is healed. I'll pay for his food.'

Cesario muttered a curse beneath his breath and strode over to his horse. For all her elfin fragility Beth was incredibly determined—and deeply compassionate, he brooded as he watched her tenderly stroke the ugly dog.

'We need to get out of the rain before we drown,' he growled. Not giving her the chance to argue, he put his hands on her waist and lifted her and the dog up onto the saddle. She was soaked to the skin and shivering. 'Take these for a second,' he ordered, dropping the reins into her hand while he shrugged out of his coat and draped it around her shoulders.

The leather coat still retained the heat from Cesario's body, and the lingering male scent of him teased Beth's senses. 'I'm already wet. It doesn't make sense for you to get soaked too,' she mumbled, but received an impatient look.

'In the space of forty-eight hours you've turned my life upside down and landed me with a baby and a flea-bitten mutt. The last thing I need now is for you to catch pneumonia,' Cesario told her grimly before he hooked his foot in the stirrup and swung himself up onto the horse's back behind her.

When they reached the castle ten minutes later, Cesario rode round to the stables, dismounted and lifted Beth down, gritting his teeth when her slender body briefly brushed against him. He bitterly resented his overwhelming awareness of her. Clearly he'd gone too long without sex, he thought sardonically. In Rome there were a number of women he could call—casual mistresses who understood he was not in the market for commitment and who would be happy to satisfy his libido knowing that he would be a generous lover in return.

Taking the dog, he strode into an empty horse box and set it down in the straw. The cut on its leg was not too deep, and while he cleaned the wound Beth knelt beside him and stroked the animal's head to keep it calm.

'Do you think he'll be okay? Poor creature. He must have been so frightened in the trap,' she said softly.

Her innate gentleness touched something deep inside Cesario. He stared at her pale fingers as she fondled the dog's ears and imagined her touching *him*, caressing his naked flesh and encircling his manhood with those delicate white hands. Her hair smelled of rain and the faint scent of lemons. His eyes were drawn lower, and through her wet blouse he could see the outline of her dusky pink nipples.

He swallowed and said roughly, 'I'm sure he'll be fine. I'll tell the groom to give him plenty of food.'

'Thank you.' Her shy smile caused a cramping sensation in Cesario's gut. But then her expression became anxious. 'I must get back to Sophie. I've been out for ages and she's bound to be awake by now.'

'She was crying before I came to look for you. But after I fed her she settled and seemed happy enough when I left her with Filomena,' Cesario told her.

'*You* fed her?' Beth chewed on her lip. 'Was she all right? I mean, she's only used to me, and…'

'She didn't choke when I gave her a bottle of formula, if that's what you mean,' Cesario said dryly. 'I'm quite capable of caring for a baby. I used to regularly feed my son.'

'You must miss your little boy.'

He stiffened at Beth's gentle comment. 'I think of him every day,' he admitted roughly.

To his relief she did not offer the unhelpful platitude that time was a great healer, as so many people did when they learned that he had lost a child. Instead, she tentatively reached out and placed her hand over his as they knelt on the stable floor next to the stray dog, and her silence soothed his ragged soul far more than meaningless words of sympathy.

'I miss Mel terribly,' she said at last. 'I feel so sad that she's not here to watch Sophie grow up.' She sighed. 'I still miss my mum, too, even though she's been dead for twelve years.'

2 Free Books!

If you have enjoyed reading this Modern™ romance book, then why not take advantage of our **FREE BOOKS OFFER**? We'll send you two books from this series absolutely **FREE** – this offer is available for a limited time only!

Accepting your FREE books places you under no obligation to buy anything.

As a member of the Mills & Boon Book Club you'll receive all these exclusive benefits:

- 🌸 FREE Home Delivery
- 🌸 Receive new titles TWO MONTHS AHEAD of the shops
- 🌸 Exclusive Special Offers & Monthly Newsletter
- 🌸 Special Rewards Programme

We hope that after receiving your free books you'll want to remain a member. But the choice is yours. So why not give us a go? You'll be glad you did!

For all the latest news and offers, why not visit

millsandboon.co.uk

Mrs/Miss/Ms/Mr .... Initials ....
BLOCK CAPITALS PLEASE

Surname ....

Address ....

....

....

.... Postcode ....

Email ....

P2EIA

The Mills & Boon® Book Club™ – Here's how it works:

Accepting your free books places you under no obligation to buy anything. You may keep the books and return the despatch note marked 'cancel'. If we do not hear from you, about a month later we'll send you **4** brand new stories from the Modern series **individually priced at £3.49* each.** That is the complete price – there is no extra charge for post and packaging. You may cancel at any time, otherwise we will send you 4 stories a month which you may purchase or return to us – the choice is yours. *Terms and prices subject to change without notice.

NO STAMP NEEDED!

MILLS
BOON®
Book Club

FREE BOOK OFFER

FREEPOST NAT 10298

RICHMOND

TW9 1BR

NO STAMP
NECESSARY
IF POSTED IN
THE U.K. OR N.I.

'You said she was ill for a long time?'

Beth nodded. 'She was diagnosed with MS when I was about five, and as her condition degenerated she wasn't able to walk and was confined to a wheelchair. She never complained, though, she just tried to get on with life. But it can't have been easy. My father had to give up work to look after her, so we didn't have much money. Mum used to get upset that I had to miss out on things like birthday parties and school trips.'

Cesario glanced at her curiously. 'You told me you became friends with Melanie Stewart when you lived in a children's home. Is your father dead too?'

'No.' She hesitated. 'He...went away. He had an affair with another woman and left Mum and me to move in with his girlfriend.'

'Dio!' Cesario did not know how to respond. As a boy he had been devastated when his mother had left the castle to be with her lover, but his feeling of abandonment was nothing compared to how Beth had surely felt at her father's callous behaviour.

'Who took care of your mother after he left?'

'I did, for a while. I didn't mind,' Beth assured him. 'I wanted to stay with Mum. But when her MS got worse she had to go into a specialist nursing home and she died soon after. Social Services asked my dad if I could live with him, but he had decided to emigrate to Australia with his new partner and didn't want me.' She gave a casual shrug, hoping to disguise the hurt she had felt at her father's rejection. 'That's when I went into care.'

She lifted her head and met Cesario's gaze. 'I don't have a great opinion of fathers. I thought you wouldn't want Sophie—just as my father didn't want me—and I only came to Sardinia because I promised Mel I would search for you. I don't want your money,' she continued fiercely. 'Even if the test proves that you are Sophie's father I don't expect anything from you. All I want is to be a mother to her.'

Beth pictured Sophie's sweet little face and she felt an ache of longing to hold the baby in her arms. She had only been away from Sophie for an hour, and already she missed her. What must it be like for Cesario to live every day missing his little boy? she thought. No wonder he seemed so grim. She understood only too well that grief felt like a lead weight inside. Most nights she still shed tears for Mel. But she sensed that Cesario kept his emotions locked deep in his heart, and his way of dealing with his pain was to ignore it.

The dog was lying quietly and appeared to be comfortable. After tucking more straw around it, Beth stood up and hurried over to the stable door. 'I must get back. I've been away from Sophie for far too long.'

Cesario also got to his feet. 'Dinner will be at eight again tonight. Teodoro will come to the nursery to escort you to the dining room.'

A shudder ran through Beth as she recalled the bitter confrontation that had taken place between them the previous evening. She was ashamed to remember how excited she had felt when she'd changed into her only nice dress in preparation for having dinner with Cesario. But he had shattered her silly romantic fantasy when he had accused her of being a thief while she had worked at Devington Hall.

She paused in the doorway and turned back to him. 'I would prefer to eat in the nursery tonight. If Filomena is too busy to serve my dinner upstairs I'll pop down to the kitchen and make a sandwich.'

Cool grey eyes trapped her gaze. 'Be ready for eight o'clock, Beth,' he murmured, in a pleasant voice that held an underlying hint of steel. 'Or I'll come and fetch you.'

His arrogance was infuriating. She felt an uncharacteristic spurt of temper and opened her mouth to argue, but the warning gleam in his eyes made her reconsider and she chose to walk away in dignified silence.

Her faithful grey skirt was beyond repair, Beth discovered later, after she had bathed and fed Sophie and settled her in her cot. She was trying to decide what to wear to dinner. Her green dress was out of the question—after the way Cesario had humiliated her last night she doubted she would ever wear it again. Her only other choice was her black skirt, which was even older than the grey one and several inches too long. Fortunately her relatively new navy blouse had been laundered and returned to her wardrobe by Carlotta. It couldn't be helped that she looked as though she was attending a funeral. She did not want Cesario to think she had dressed to impress him, she reminded herself, as she pulled her hair back from her face and secured it in a tight knot on top of her head.

Teodoro was waiting for her when she stepped out of the nursery, and as she followed him down the stairs she was conscious of her heart thumping erratically beneath her ribs. Just as on the previous evening, Cesario was already in the dining room, looking dangerously sexy in tailored black trousers and a white silk shirt open at the throat to reveal a vee of olive-gold skin and a smattering of black hairs that Beth knew from the night of the landslide covered his chest and arrowed down over his abdomen.

She felt a rush of nervousness when Teodoro left the room and closed the door behind him, leaving her alone with the enigmatic master of the Castello del Falco. She wished he would speak, or give one of his rare smiles, but he subjected her to a silent, intent scrutiny, his eyes lingering on the pulse thudding at the base of her throat.

'Did you think you could hide your beauty from me by dressing like a nun?' he demanded harshly. 'Or were you hoping that your drab attire would quash my desire for you? If so, you were mistaken.' He reached out a hand, and before Beth realised his intention he released the clip that secured her chignon so that her hair tumbled in a stream of brown silk down her back.

'How dare you?' Her shocked response died on her lips as he slid his hand beneath her hair and cupped her nape, exerting gentle force to draw her inexorably closer to him. His eyes glittered like tensile steel, but she recognised the savage hunger in their depths and trembled as the memory of how he had kissed her in the rain flooded her mind.

All the time she had been bathing and playing with Sophie after she had returned to the castle she had determinedly not allowed herself to think about the wild passion that had exploded between her and Cesario. But now, as she stared at his hard-boned face, she was consumed by a primitive urgency for him to crush her against his chest and claim her mouth with fierce possession.

As his head slowly lowered she held her breath. She trembled with longing to feel his lips slide over hers, for his tongue to probe between them, demanding access to the moist interior of her mouth. Mindlessly, she swayed towards him, but to her shame and dismay he stiffened and jerked his head back, as if he was determined to fight the sexual alchemy that smouldered between them.

'Let's eat,' he said curtly, and he stepped away from her and held out a chair for her to sit down at the table.

'Filomena has left food on the hot-plate so that we can serve ourselves. What would you like to drink?'

'Lemonade, please.' Somehow Beth managed to make her voice sound normal and act as if she was unaffected by Cesario, even though inside she was shaking with reaction to him. She could not risk drinking wine tonight, when it was imperative she keep a clear head, she thought desperately.

She ate the starter of fish soup without fully appreciating its delicate flavour. To follow, Cesario served her a plate of round-shaped pasta, similar to ravioli, which Beth discovered was filled with potato and mint and was accompanied by a tomato and basil sauce.

'The dish is called *sa fregula* and is a traditional Sardinian recipe,' he explained, when she tasted the pasta and commented on its delicious flavour. He took a sip of his red wine and glanced across the table at her. 'Teodoro told me you were asking him about the history of the castle?'

Relieved that their conversation seemed to be avoiding her personal life, Beth nodded. 'It's such a fascinating place. How old did you say it is?'

'The original building dates back to the thirteenth century. Over time it was extended, and in more recent years modern additions such as electricity and a better plumbing system were installed. I imagine my ancestors did not bathe very often when water had to be drawn from the well and carried to the bedchambers on the upper floors of the castle,' he said, amusement glinting in his eyes.

He went on to tell her more about the history of the Castello del Falco, and Beth gradually relaxed, intrigued by his stories and seduced by his deep, accented voice that caressed her senses like velvet against her skin.

'It's amazing to think of people living here hundreds of years ago,' she murmured, surprised to realise that while she had been listening to him she had eaten the whole plate of food he had served her.

'The Nuragic civilisation is known to have lived on Sardinia much longer ago than mere hundreds of years,' he said, handing her a cup of coffee. 'The landscape is dotted with more than seven thousand ancient stone structures called Nuraghi. Archaeologists believe they were built round about the fifteenth century BC and they are thought to have been homesteads of communities who lived in the Bronze Age.'

Beth's eyes widened. 'And the buildings are still standing today? I'd love to see them.'

'Many have become ruins over time, of course, but the basic structures remain. There is a settlement called Serra Orrios close to Oliena, at Dorgali, and also an ancient tomb called the Giant's Grave of Thomes which, as the name suggests, is believed to have been a burial chamber.' His smile held genuine warmth at her enthusiasm. 'Perhaps there will be time while you are staying here for you to visit Dorgali.'

Beth's stomach dipped at his words which were a stark reminder that the length of her stay at the castle was determined by when the DNA test could be done. If Mel had been wrong and Cesario wasn't Sophie's father she would take the baby back to England. But if Sophie was his— what would happen then? she wondered fearfully.

Desperate for something to say, she glanced around the room at the many paintings that lined the walls. One portrait in particular, of a stern-faced man dressed in modern-day clothes, caught her attention.

'My father,' Cesario told her, following her gaze.

'He looks…' Beth hesitated, wishing she had not started the conversation. 'Very aristocratic.'

'He was a cold, remote man.' Cesario stared at the portrait. 'I was terrified of him when I was a child. He was never physically violent towards me,' he explained, when Beth looked horrified, 'but there are other forms of cruelty. He believed that Piras men should never feel emotions and certainly never reveal them.'

He gave a sardonic laugh. 'You see the pennant hanging on the wall, decorated with the family crest of two swords? The translation of my family motto is "Victory and Power are All". For my father the Piras name and the pursuit of power were all he cared about, and he was determined to instil those values into me.'

'What about your mother?' Beth asked, trying to hide her shock at Cesario's revelations about his upbringing by the man whose austere features were staring down at her from above the fireplace. Teodoro had told her that Cesario's father had died several years ago, but the butler had not mentioned his mother. 'Her portrait isn't in here,' she noted, realising that the only paintings of women hanging in the dining room were probably a few hundred years old.

'No, my father had every trace of her removed from the castle when she ended their marriage. When I was seven years old I came home from boarding school, excited at the prospect of seeing her. But she had gone without even saying goodbye and I never saw her again.'

'Didn't she ever visit you, or invite you to her new home?'

He shook his head. 'My father paid her a large sum of money in return for her agreement to sign sole custody of me over to him. When I asked my father if I could see her he told me what he had done, and I swear he took pleasure in explaining that my mother had preferred money to her only child.' His mouth curled into a mirthless smile. 'It was a salutary life lesson,' he said harshly.

Beneath his sardonic tone Beth glimpsed the hurt young boy he had once been. She glanced at the portrait of his grim-faced father and her heart softened towards Cesario. Rejection by a parent was something she had experienced too, and she wondered if, like her, Cesario found it hard to trust. Some parents, like her mother, were wonderful role models, she mused. But others, like her father and both of Cesario's parents, could cause untold harm to a child's emotional stability.

'Not all women are like that,' she said quietly. 'Not all women think money is more important than a loving relationship.'

'Is that so?' Cesario drawled cynically, casting his mind over past affairs he'd had with women who had regarded his wealth as his main attraction. Yet he knew there was some truth in Beth's words. He had never considered offering to pay Raffaella off, as his father had done his mother. Raffaella had loved Nicolo, but her desperate bid to snatch him from the castle had resulted in tragedy.

The peal of the castle's internal phone shattered the tense silence that had fallen in the dining room. Cesario stood up and strode across the room to answer it. 'Sophie is awake,' he relayed a few moments later. 'Carlotta can't settle her.'

'She's due a feed.' Beth glanced at her watch and was shocked to see how late it was. The hours she'd spent with Cesario had flown by, and even more startling was the realisation that she had enjoyed his company. She felt guilty that she had forgotten about Sophie's 11:00 p.m. feed and jumped up from the table.

Cesario opened the door and followed her out of the dining room. 'I'll escort you up to the nursery. I doubt you can remember the way yet through the rabbit warren of corridors.'

Sophie's cries could be heard as they walked along the first-floor landing. As soon as they reached the nursery Beth hurried over to the cot and lifted the red-faced, sobbing baby into her arms.

'It's all right, sweetheart, I'm here now,' she soothed, her guilt that she had left Sophie again for a few hours increasing when she discovered that the baby's sleepsuit was wet. She deftly stripped off the wet suit, changed Sophie's nappy and popped her into clean nightwear, working quickly while the baby yelled indignantly at having to wait for her milk.

'Is her formula ready?' Cesario queried.

'No.' Beth groaned. 'I need to make up a couple of feeds for the night.'

'Let me take her while you prepare her bottle.'

As he cradled Sophie against his chest Cesario felt a strange sensation inside him, as if tight bindings around his heart were slowly unravelling. He did not know if she was his child but it did not seem important. All that mattered was that he comforted her, and he murmured to her in Italian the lullaby *'Stella Stellina'*—Star, Little Star—that he had often sung to his son.

Sophie stopped crying and focused her big brown eyes on him. If she was his daughter he would love her as he had loved Nicolo, Cesario vowed fiercely. But what would he do about Sophie's guardian? Beth had convinced him with her utter devotion to the baby that she loved Sophie as much as if she were her own child. It would not be fair to send her away.

Perhaps he could employ her as Sophie's nanny? he brooded. That way they could both be part of the baby's life. But he did not relish the idea of Beth living at the castle while he was plagued by this damnable fascination with her. She had only been here for two days and he was racked with an unprecedented hunger to possess her slender body.

In many ways it would be easier if Sophie was not his. That way he could send Beth back to England with a clear conscience and get on with his life. No doubt he would soon forget her once she could no longer cast her siren spell over him with her slanting green eyes, he thought self-derisively.

The sound of her voice dragged him from his thoughts. 'I knew you had a magic touch,' she said as she emerged from the small kitchen area adjoining the nursery, holding a bottle of baby formula. 'Nothing normally pacifies Sophie when she's due a feed.'

The way Sophie responded to Cesario was uncanny, Beth thought when he carefully transferred the baby into her arms and she settled down in a chair to feed her. Was it possible that she somehow sensed Cesario was her father? Was it blood calling to blood? And if that was true then surely Sophie belonged here at the Castello del Falco.

Sophie was almost asleep by the time she had finished her milk, and after laying her in the cot Beth walked over to the window where Cesario was standing, looking out at the impenetrable darkness that cloaked the castle and the surrounding mountains.

'I think she'll settle now—until she wakes for her early-morning feed,' she murmured, feeling her heart give a little flip when she glanced at him and found that he had turned his head and he was watching her with an indefinable expression in his grey eyes.

'You should get to bed too, after your eventful day. I hear you've sweet-talked Filomena into allowing your dog to sleep in her kitchen?'

She flushed and gave him an anxious look, relieved to see amusement in his eyes rather than annoyance. 'Harry was lonely on his own in the stables.'

Dark brows winged upwards. 'Harry?'

'I had to call him something,' Beth said defensively. 'When I was a little girl we had a dog called Harry who I loved to bits. But my father said he had enough to do looking after my mother and he sold him.' She sighed. 'Filomena says her sister might give Harry a home. I won't be able to take him back to England with me, and it wouldn't be fair to keep a dog in a one-bedroom flat on the fifth floor.'

'It doesn't sound an ideal place to bring up a child, either.'

She bit her lip. 'No, it isn't. If it turns out that Sophie is not your child, I'll apply to the local council to see if we can be rehoused. Somewhere with a garden for her to play in would be nice.' She thought of the beautiful castle gardens and imagined Sophie as a toddler, running across the grass. 'But there's a long waiting list for housing in London.'

'Agreeing to be the guardian of your friend's baby was a huge undertaking,' Cesario said brusquely. 'You are young and you have your whole life ahead of you—a career, relationships. You have sacrificed the independent life you could have had to bring up another woman's child.'

'My life is different, certainly, but I don't regard having Sophie a sacrifice. I love her more than anything, and I intend to do everything I can to give her a happy childhood.'

Beth gave a faintly wistful smile. 'When I was a little girl I dreamed of being a ballerina. I was desperate to go to ballet classes like the other girls at school, but Mum couldn't afford it—especially after my father left us. When Sophie is older I want her to have the opportunity to do everything she wants to do.'

Cesario dragged his gaze from Beth's earnest face and resumed his contemplation of the night sky, where silver stars were now pinpricking the velvet blackness.

'You have a ridiculously soft heart, Beth Granger,' he said roughly. He paused. 'So who planted Alicia Devington's diamond earrings in your room?'

Beth gave him a startled look. In the darkened nursery his profile seemed all angles and planes, and the glimmering moonlight flickering over his scar made him look as harsh and unyielding as his ancestors who had once strode along the battlements of the Castello del Falco.

She swallowed, before replying shakily, 'Hugo Devington.'

His head swivelled round and he pierced her with an intent stare. 'Why would Hugo Devington have wanted you to appear to be a thief?'

'Because he needed a reason to sack me after I'd threatened to—' She broke off and stared down at her fingers as she twisted them together, sickened by unpleasant memories that she had spent the past six months trying to forget. She sensed Cesario's impatience and forced herself to continue. 'After I threatened to tell Mrs Devington that her husband had tried to…assault me.'

'What do you mean by assault?'

Colour flared on her cheeks. 'Sexually,' she muttered.

'*Santa Madre!* You mean he raped you?' Cesario felt a violent urge to find Hugo Devington and tear him limb from limb.

'No—it didn't get that far. At first he just used to make comments about my body, and if I ever happened to be alone in a room with him he would stand too close and…' her blush deepened '…pat me on the bottom, but then make a joke of it.'

She sighed. 'I didn't know what to do, so I just tried to keep out of his way. But then one evening, when Mrs Devington was out, he called me into his study, saying he wanted to discuss one of his sons.' She unconsciously twisted her fingers tighter together, unaware that Cesario had noted the betraying sign of her distress. 'Well, to cut a long story short, he tried to kiss me. I pushed him away, of course, and then he got angry and grabbed me. He put his hand up my skirt and tried to…touch me. I managed to fight him off, but he came after me, and so I threatened that I would tell his wife what he had done. I hoped that would be the end of it—that he wouldn't try anything again—but the next day Mrs Devington's earrings went missing, and when she searched the house she found them in my room. She wanted to call the police and have me arrested, but Hugo stopped her and said it would be better if I was sacked and left Devington Hall immediately.'

'Why didn't *you* insist that the police were called?' Cesario demanded. 'You hadn't stolen the earrings, so why didn't you try to defend yourself? Why didn't you report to the police that Devington had sexually assaulted you?'

'I had no proof. No one would have believed my word over that of a famous barrister. *You* didn't believe me,' she reminded him.

'Last night I wasn't aware of all the facts.' He looked uncomfortable. 'I owe you an apology. I'd just received a report from my private investigator and I had no reason not to believe that what he'd heard about you was true.'

Beth bit her lip. 'Why do you believe me now? I could be lying.'

Cesario studied her elfin features. Her pale, almost translucent skin was bare of make-up and her silky brown hair was beautifully natural. There was no artifice about her, and he wondered with a jolt if her virginal air could also be real.

'You wear your honesty like a badge,' he said roughly. 'Your emotions are transparent—your love for Sophie, your kindness to an injured animal. I don't think you are capable of lying either by word or action.'

His voice deepened, and the seductive huskiness in his tone sent a quiver through Beth. He was watching her through half-closed lids and the searing intensity of his gaze made her catch her breath.

'Your body did not lie when I kissed you. I felt the sweet urgency of your response.' He framed her face with his hands and gently stroked her hair behind her ears before he traced the fragile line of her jaw. 'You are as much a prisoner of this damnable desire that burns between us as I am, *mia bella*.'

She could not deny it—not when his mouth was so close to hers that his warm breath whispered across her lips. She wanted him to kiss her so desperately that her whole body trembled, and when he closed the few inches that separated his mouth from hers a soft sigh escaped her and she parted her lips with an innocent eagerness that caused Cesario's gut to clench.

It was different from when he had kissed her in the rain.

He was different...gentler; his hands shook a little as he slid them from her face to her throat and then traced the delicate line of her collarbone. He brushed his mouth over hers in a sensual tasting with an underlying tenderness that she found utterly beguiling. Slowly, like a flower unfurling in response to sunlight, she began to kiss him back, tentatively at first. But at his low groan of approval she grew bolder and parted her mouth so that he could explore her with his tongue.

'Beth,' he said in a low, urgent voice, as his restraint cracked and he pulled her up against his hard body. His arms tightened around her, one hand tangling in her hair as he angled her head and plundered her mouth with feverish passion.

She responded to him mindlessly, straining her slender body against him and lifting her hands to his face to ensure that he kept his lips on hers. The dark stubble shading his jaw felt abrasive beneath her fingertips. She gently traced the scar that sliced down his cheek and felt him stiffen, but after a moment the tension seemed to drain from him and he deepened the kiss, taking it to another level so that it became a flagrant ravishment of her senses.

Her heart-rate quickened when he slid his hand down from her shoulder to her breast and cupped the small mound in his palm. She could feel the warmth of his skin through her blouse and felt an intense longing for him to undo the buttons and slip his hand inside her bra to touch her bare flesh.

An image flashed into her mind of his darkly tanned fingers curled possessively around her pale breasts, and she shivered with a mixture of anticipation and faint trepidation. No man had ever seen her unclothed before, or caressed her naked body. But Cesario must have made love to dozens of women, perhaps hundreds, she thought, remembering how Mel had described him as a womaniser.

From the cot came a tiny murmur, little more than a sigh as Sophie changed position in her sleep. But the sound shattered the sensual spell that had held Beth enthralled and she tore her mouth from Cesario's, shaking like a leaf blown in a storm as she snatched air into her lungs.

'No…I can't do this,' she told him in a panicky voice.

What was she *doing*? her brain demanded. How could she contemplate giving her body to a man who had had a one-night stand with her best friend and who was very possibly the father of Mel's baby?

Cesario's eyes narrowed, but he dropped his hands to his sides and frowned when she immediately jerked back from him.

'What's the matter?' His nostrils flared as he fought to control his frustration. His body throbbed with sexual anticipation and the only thought in his head was how desperately he wanted to carry Beth to his room, remove her clothes and position himself between her slim thighs. But the wariness in her eyes forced him to exert formidable will-power over his rampant desire.

He recalled how she had told him that her previous employer had tried to sexually assault her and he felt sick to his stomach. 'Are you *afraid* of me?' he grated.

'No.' Beth shook her head. Cesario sounded appalled, and she instinctively wanted to reassure him. 'Not of you.' She swallowed. 'But of myself…of this.'

His assessment of her character had been correct. She could not lie even to protect her pride.

She gave a helpless shrug, unable to put into words how much he overwhelmed her. 'We are little more than strangers,' she said shakily. 'If it wasn't for Sophie we would never have met.' She held his gaze and continued quietly. 'You say you desire me, but perhaps you simply want a woman—any woman—to temporarily share your bed. And I am convenient, like Mel was.'

Cesario fought a strong urge to snatch her back into his arms and shake some sense into her, then kiss her sense-less to prove beyond doubt that he desired her more than any woman he had ever met. But essentially she was right in her guess that he would only ever want a brief affair, he acknowledged. He doubted his hunger for her would be satisfied by taking her to bed for one night, but he did not want a long-term relationship, and his interest in his mistresses invariably waned after a few weeks.

And then there was Sophie to consider—the child who might be his, even though he had no memory of her mother. It was little wonder that Beth was regarding him with deep mistrust in her expressive green eyes.

Another whimper came from the cot. Beth tensed. 'You should go,' she whispered. 'We're disturbing her.'

Cesario's mouth twisted as he envisaged the long night ahead of him. It promised to be hell when he was burning up for this pale English rose who could arouse him with one look or one glimpse of her shy smile. But she was right, of course. Sophie must come before any other con-sideration.

He nodded tersely and forced himself to move away from her. 'Sleep well, then, Beth—if you can,' he said sar-donically, before he turned and strode out of the nursery.

CHAPTER SEVEN

THE sky was a cloudless azure blue when Beth opened the curtains the following morning, and despite her tiredness after another sleepless night when her thoughts had been dominated by Cesario she felt her spirits lift.

'Look,' she murmured to Sophie, holding the baby up to the window. 'The mountains are so clear it's as if you could reach out and touch them.'

Sophie gurgled happily at the sound of her voice and continued to investigate Beth's ear with her finger.

'You are adorable—do you know that?' A wave of intense love swept through Beth as she rested her cheek against the baby's silky-soft hair. Sophie had inherited her mother's dark brown eyes, and Beth felt a sudden rush of tears as she was swamped with memories of Mel.

'One day I'll tell you all about your mummy,' she murmured. 'She was the best friend anyone could have. She wanted you so much, and she would have loved you with all her heart—just as I do.'

She changed Sophie's nappy, and was just fastening the buttons on one of the pretty little dresses that her neighbour Maureen in England had passed on, after her granddaughter had outgrown it, when the maid came into the nursery.

'What are you doing?' she queried in a puzzled voice when Carlotta opened a drawer, took out Sophie's sleep-suits and packed them in the nappy bag.

'You go. You and *bambina*.' Carlotta made a valiant attempt to speak English. 'Signor Piras say you leave now. This day.'

'I see.' Heart thumping, Beth scooped up Sophie and hurried out of the nursery. Had Cesario decided not to go ahead with the DNA test and was now sending her and Sophie home? And, if so, had he made that decision because she had called a halt to their passion the previous night?

As she reached the bottom of the staircase he emerged from his study and strode across the hall to meet her. Today the devil-may-care pirate had been transformed into a suave billionaire banker. Dressed in an impeccably tailored charcoal-grey suit, pale blue shirt and navy tie, he was to die for, Beth thought weakly. Even his unruly black hair had been tamed a little. But his veneer of sophistication could not disguise his dominant masculinity. He was formidably powerful and undoubtedly ruthless.

Those granite grey eyes above his slashing cheekbones were as hard as steel as he subjected her to an unsparing scrutiny, noting the soft flush of colour that briefly stained her pale face when her gaze met his.

'Why is Carlotta packing Sophie's things? She said that we are to leave the castle.'

'I have meetings scheduled at the Piras-Cossu Bank today and I've decided that you and Sophie should come to Rome with me. I've contacted a clinic who will carry out the DNA test there. The results should be back within two weeks. I'm sure you agree that the sooner we know the truth of Sophie's parentage the better,' he said coolly.

Beth tried to ignore her feeling of dread that if the test proved Cesario was Sophie's father he would demand custody of her. 'Has the landslide been cleared already?' She had assumed that they would be trapped at the castle for several days.

'No, but the weather has improved, which means that my helicopter can land in the castle grounds. The rain and thick cloud of the last few days made visibility too poor to fly,' he explained when she gave him a startled look.

'I'm not taking Sophie on a helicopter.' The flight on a commercial jet to Sardinia had been nerve-racking enough. It had been the first time Beth had flown and she hadn't enjoyed the experience.

'It's perfectly safe,' Cesario assured her. 'I regularly commute to Rome by helicopter.'

He turned his attention to Sophie and gave her a gentle smile. To Beth's surprise the baby, who was usually reticent with strangers, smiled back and held out her arms to him.

'Come on, *piccola*,' he murmured, his stern features softening as he lifted her and held her against his shoulder. He strode out of the front door, but paused on the steps and glanced back impatiently at Beth. 'We need to leave.' He skimmed his eyes over her and added in an amused voice, 'I see you've dressed to audition for a role in *The Sound of Music*.'

Beth felt a spurt of temper which made her forget her worries about flying. She was well aware that her black skirt was too long and the grey tee shirt too drab. She did not need him to remind her that she was a non-starter in the fashion stakes. 'I don't own many clothes,' she snapped, as she followed him across the courtyard to where the helicopter was waiting.

'That is something else we will take care of while we are in Rome,' he murmured obliquely.

There was no chance for her to ask him what he meant while the pilot helped her climb into the helicopter and instructed her to fasten her seat belt. She glanced around the luxurious cabin, at the cream leather seats and polished walnut fitments, including a small drinks bar, and ruefully compared it to the cramped economy seats on the budget airline plane she had flown on to Sardinia. Nothing emphasised Cesario's billionaire status more acutely than this private helicopter. She did not belong in his rarefied world of the super-rich, she acknowledged heavily. But if Sophie was his child she would have no right to deny the little girl the privileged life Cesario could give her.

Her heart was in her mouth when the helicopter took off, and she closed her eyes so that she could not see the ground growing farther and farther away.

'Try to relax,' Cesario said softly, no hint of teasing in his deep voice. He curled his big hand over hers. 'If you look to your right you can see Lake Cedrino, and over there that high peak is Monte Corrasi, one of the highest mountains in Sardinia.'

The view was breathtaking, Beth discovered, when she warily lifted her lashes. Cesario continued to point out various places of interest and her tension gradually eased—although she was not as relaxed as Sophie, who had fallen asleep in her baby seat.

Soon they were flying over the coast and across the sea towards mainland Italy. 'We should be in Rome in twenty minutes,' Cesario told her after a while. 'We'll go straight to my apartment. I've arranged for a representative from the clinic to meet us there, so that he can take mouth swabs for the DNA test.'

'I don't see why it was necessary for me and Sophie to come with you.' Beth had been puzzling over his decision for most of the flight. 'Couldn't you have arranged for the person from the clinic to have flown to the castle?'

'I could have done. But I have another reason for bringing you to Rome.' At her enquiring look he continued, 'I have tickets for the ballet. The Teatro dell'Opera di Roma orchestra and ballet company are putting on a production of *Romeo and Juliet*. Tonight is the opening night and I thought you might like to come with me.'

'I've never been to the ballet—I've only ever watched it on TV.' Beth quickly quashed her spurt of excitement. 'But if you have already booked the tickets surely you must have planned to take someone else? You can't disappoint your...' she hesitated, wondering about the identity of the other person '...friend by taking me instead.'

Cesario shrugged. 'My guest can no longer come, so her ticket is available. It would be a shame to waste it.'

'I see.' An inexplicable feeling of jealousy seared Beth's insides as she guessed that Cesario had intended to take his mistress to the ballet. No doubt the woman was gorgeous and sophisticated, as suited Italy's most eligible billionaire banker. 'I'd better not come,' she said stiffly. 'It might make things awkward between you and your girlfriend.'

Cesario heard the disappointment in her voice and was tempted to shake her—or kiss her. Kissing her was definitely the preferable option, he acknowledged as his gaze lingered on her soft pink mouth.

'I don't have a current girlfriend. I bought the ticket for my PA, as a thank-you for the hard work she does for me, but something has come up and she is no longer free tonight.'

It was only a little white lie, Cesario assured himself.

He was *not* going to admit that, after Beth had told him last night about how she had longed for ballet lessons when she was a child, he had phoned one of his contacts and told him to get hold of tickets for tonight's performance, whatever the cost.

Cesario was searching for something in his briefcase, but Beth had the strangest feeling that he was avoiding looking at her. 'Come with me tonight if you want to,' he said casually. 'I thought you said you liked ballet. But if you're not interested…'

'Oh, I am. I'd love to come.' Another thought struck Beth. 'But what about Sophie? I can't leave her, and I'm sure babies aren't welcome at the opera house.'

'Don't worry. Everything is arranged. Sophie will be well cared for while we are out.'

While they had been talking the helicopter had flown over the city, and now it began to descend towards a helipad on the roof of a high-rise building. Beth's nervousness returned, and she was so intent on gripping her seat that she could barely hear Cesario's assurance, or question why he had arranged a babysitter before he had known she was to accompany him to the theatre.

The helicopter landed on the roof of the Piras-Cossu Bank's head offices in the business district of Rome. Beth had a fleeting impression of grey-carpeted corridors, plush offices and lots of tinted glass, before a lift swept them to the ground floor, where they crossed a marble foyer and stepped outside to climb into a waiting limousine.

Cesario's apartment overlooked a *piazza* called the *Campo de' Fiori*, which he explained meant field of flowers, where a busy market selling fruit, vegetables and flowers operated every morning. The outside of the apartment block was a beautiful historic building, but to Beth's surprise inside the penthouse flat was modern and starkly minimalist, with white marble floors, white walls and furnishings.

'Your city home is very different to the castle,' she commented, privately thinking that the apartment seemed as sterile and unwelcoming as a clinic.

'It's not to my taste. My wife chose the décor. Raffaella disliked the castle and preferred to spend her time in Rome, but for me the flat is simply somewhere to stay when I need to be at the bank. I've never bothered to have it redecorated.'

Cesario had carried Sophie up from the car, but now he gave her to Beth before ushering her into the lounge. Two men were waiting there, and after speaking to them in Italian Cesario introduced the younger man as a representative from a paternity testing clinic, while the older, white-haired man, he explained, was a doctor.

'Obtaining a DNA sample is done by taking a mouth swab and is absolutely painless,' the clinic rep assured Beth. 'I will take a sample from Signor Piras first, and then from the child.'

Sophie seemed quite unconcerned, and the test was performed in minutes. But Beth felt tense as the sample was taken which would prove whether or not Cesario was Sophie's father. If he wasn't, then she would take Mel's baby daughter back to Hackney, to the cramped flat in the run-down tower block. She would manage, she told herself. Hopefully she'd find a better-paid job which would enable her to afford somewhere nicer for them to live. But it was unlikely she would ever see Cesario again.

The thought hurt more than it should. Why should she care? she wondered despairingly. He was all but a stranger—a wealthy playboy whose world was so different from hers that they might as well live on different planets. She stole a glance at him and felt an ache inside as she drank in his hard, handsome features, and the cruel scar running down his cheek that gave him the faintest air of vulnerability and proved he was made of flesh and blood, not carved from granite. He was the only man to have kissed her with fierce passion and awoken her desires, to have made her long for him to possess her body and take her to the heights of sexual fulfilment.

Her heart leapt when he turned his head and trapped her gaze, his expression speculative as he watched the streaks of colour wing along her cheekbones.

'You will be contacted with the results as soon as they are available,' the clinic rep explained after he had sealed the samples, and with a polite nod he walked out of the room.

To Beth's surprise, the doctor did not follow. She had assumed his role had been to witness the collection of the DNA sample, but Cesario explained otherwise.

'I've asked Dr Bartoli to examine you, in the hope that he can diagnose why you keep fainting,' he told her.

'You make it sound as though it's a regular occurrence,' she muttered in an angry whisper so that the doctor could not hear her. 'I just feel a bit wobbly sometimes. There's nothing wrong with me and I don't need to see a doctor.'

'Why don't you let him be the judge of that?' The determined gleam in Cesario's eyes warned that she would be wasting her time to argue, and she glared at him helplessly as he took Sophie from her and strolled over to the window.

'So, Signorina Granger, would you please tell me the symptoms you have been suffering from?'

Beth forced a smile for the elderly doctor. He spoke in

such a kind tone that she shrugged and admitted, 'I sometimes feel dizzy and short of breath. And I'm often tired. But Sophie still wakes for a feed during the night so I suppose it's not surprising that I feel exhausted.'

'Caring for an infant can be extremely draining, especially in the first few months,' the doctor agreed. 'It is important that you eat a good, balanced diet to give you energy.'

When Beth flushed, remembering the days she had survived on toast and coffee in England, he continued, 'I understand you are the child's guardian, and that her mother was your best friend who died shortly after Sophie's birth?' He gave her a gentle look. 'Grief takes a physical as well as mental toll. Perhaps you have lost your appetite since the death of your friend? And perhaps,' he added intuitively, 'you have been so busy caring for the baby that you have not had time to grieve properly.'

'No.' Beth swallowed hard. She had a sudden stark memory of Mel's funeral, the utter wrench she'd felt as she'd said that final goodbye. Tears filled her eyes and for a moment she felt like sobbing her heart out. But of course she couldn't—not in front of a stranger. Anyway, she had learned after her mother had died that crying wasn't really a relief. It just gave you a headache. And how could she wallow in self-pity when Sophie needed her to be strong?

'The past few months have been difficult,' she admitted huskily.

She was conscious that on the other side of the room Cesario was listening to her conversation. She felt his eyes on her, but she could not bring herself to meet his gaze when she felt so vulnerable.

'I think from what you have told me, and also from your pallor, that you are probably suffering from an iron deficiency,' Dr Bartoli told her. 'I will take a blood sample to confirm it, but it will do no harm for you to start a course of iron tablets immediately.'

Five minutes later the doctor packed the small phial containing Beth's blood sample in his medical bag and shook her hand. '*Arrivederci, signorina.* It is important you take care of yourself. I do not underestimate how hard life can be for a single mother.'

Cesario escorted Dr Bartoli out of the lounge. When he returned moments later he was accompanied by a woman who Beth assumed was a member of his staff at the apartment.

'Beth, I'd like you to meet Luisa Moretti. Luisa is a nanny from a highly reputable agency in Rome,' he shocked her by saying. 'She is going to help you look after Sophie.'

'I'm pleased to meet you, Miss Granger.' The woman spoke perfect English and smiled as she extended her hand in formal greeting. Good manners dictated that Beth responded with a polite welcome, but while Luisa made a fuss of Sophie she glared at Cesario.

To her fury he returned her angry look with a bland smile before speaking to the nanny. 'Beth and I have an appointment, and as Sophie is due a feed and a nap we'll leave her with you for a couple of hours.'

'Sophie won't like being fed by a stranger,' Beth said stiffly, but to no avail.

'I'm sure she'll be quite happy with me,' Luisa assured her. 'I've worked as a nanny for twenty years, and I have a lot of experience with small babies.'

With Cesario's hand firmly gripping her shoulder, Beth found herself propelled out of the room. Before she could speak, he answered a call on his mobile phone, and she had no opportunity to vent her feelings until they had climbed into the limousine parked outside the apartment block.

'Don't think I don't realise what you are doing.' She rounded on him the second he'd depressed a button to activate the privacy glass so that the chauffeur could not hear them. 'You believe Sophie is your daughter, and once the test proves it you're planning to send me away from her. That's why you've employed a nanny. But I *won't* leave her,' she told him fiercely. 'Mel appointed me as Sophie's guardian, and I'll fight you in court if necessary for the right to be a mother to her.'

Her emotions were raw after her conversation with the doctor had triggered painful memories of Mel, and now the tears she had tried to supress filled her eyes.

The sight of Beth's distress made Cesario's stomach clench. 'You're wrong,' he said tautly. 'I've employed Luisa because you've admitted you are exhausted from lack of sleep and I can see that you need help. *Dio*, your devotion to her has made you ill. If Sophie is mine, I promise I will involve you in her upbringing.'

What did he mean by that? Beth wondered anxiously. Would Cesario allow her to live at the Castello del Falco? Or would her involvement in Sophie's life be confined to occasional visits? Gnawing on her lower lip, she stared out of the car window at the traffic-congested streets and the unfamiliar Rome skyline. 'Where are we going, anyway?'

'Shopping—we need to find you a dress to wear tonight.'

She shook her head. '*We* do not. The clothes I'm wearing might not be haute couture, but they're adequate. I can't afford to buy a dress that I'll probably never have the opportunity to wear again, and I'm certainly not going to allow you to buy me anything.'

'*Mio Dio!* You would try the patience of a saint—and that is something I have never professed to be,' Cesario growled.

Something in his tone made Beth's heart thud. When she darted him a glance and saw the feral gleam in his eyes she should have guessed his intention. Certainly she should have fought him when his arm snaked around her waist and he hauled her up against him. But the memory of his kiss was branded on her soul, and when he claimed her mouth with savage possession she lost the battle before it had even begun. For a few seconds she fought him, determined to resist his mastery, but he took without mercy, parting her lips with determined intent to explore her inner sweetness with his tongue.

Driven by a need she did not fully understand, Beth responded to him with an urgency that made him groan. Sensing her surrender, Cesario gentled the kiss so that it became deeply sensual, with an inherent tenderness that caused her tears that had been hovering perilously close since they had climbed into the car to overspill.

'Don't,' he bade her roughly, brushing the trails of moisture from her cheeks with his thumb pads. 'I know how much you love Sophie, and whatever the outcome of the test I swear you will never be parted from her.'

'If the test proves that you are her father you said you will want her to grow up in Sardinia with you. But my home is in England. How can we both be parents to her when we live in different countries?'

It would be so much easier if Sophie wasn't Cesario's child, Beth thought wearily. But she knew she was being selfish. Undoubtedly it would be better for Sophie if she were the daughter of a billionaire.

'We'll work something out,' Cesario reassured her.

In truth he did not know what, but Beth's fear that she might be separated from the child she patently adored tugged on his heart. Guilt surged through him as he remembered Raffaella's desperation to win custody of Nicolo—and his determination to keep his son. There had been no winners in their bitter battle, he thought grimly.

He stared at Beth's tense face and drew her close so that her head rested on his shoulder. 'I give you my word that you will always have a place in Sophie's life.'

Like every room in the penthouse, the nursery's décor was stark white. It was probably very stylish, but in Beth's opinion it lacked the cosy charm of the nursery at the Castello del Falco. Sophie, however, seemed oblivious to her surroundings, and had fallen asleep soon after her evening feed.

Feeling the familiar surge of love for the baby girl, Beth leant over the cot and brushed a tender kiss on Sophie's petal-soft cheek.

'She took her whole bottle and settled without a murmur,' Luisa Moretti told her in a hushed voice. 'I'll take good care of her while you are out, so please don't worry about her.' The nanny smiled. 'What a beautiful dress, Miss Granger.'

'Please call me Beth.' Luisa was so friendly that Beth had quickly warmed to her, and if she was honest it *was* a relief to share a little of the responsibility of caring for Sophie with a highly experienced nanny.

She glanced at her reflection in the mirror and gave a rueful laugh. 'It's an amazing dress, isn't it? But I've never worn red in my life and I'm not sure I can carry it off.'

She had voiced her doubts earlier in the day to the stylist Cesario had arranged to accompany her on a shopping trip on the Via dei Condotti—reputed to be one of the richest streets in Rome—where all the top designer boutiques could be found. The stylist had persuaded her to try on dozens of outfits but, horrified by the price tags, Beth had refused to buy anything with the credit card Cesario had given her and had only reluctantly agreed to the red dress because she had been impatient to get back to Sophie.

'With your slim figure, the dress looks stunning on you,' the stylist had insisted.

A trip to the hair and beauty salon had followed, and to her surprise Beth had enjoyed the novel experience of being pampered.

'I can't believe I look so glamorous,' she told Luisa, as she studied her glossy hair with its new wispy layers that framed her face. The stylist had suggested she wear slightly more make-up for the evening, and had emphasised her eyes with a smoky shadow and brushed a light red gloss over her lips. Silver stiletto sandals and purse completed the outfit, and with a last glance in the mirror she went to find Cesario.

He was waiting for her in the lounge: tall, dark and devastatingly sexy in a black dinner suit and white silk shirt. Beth paused in the doorway and her heart-rate accelerated when he looked over at her and visibly tensed. His eyes narrowed, but as he walked towards her she was conscious of the feral gleam beneath his heavy lids.

'*Bellissima!* You take my breath away,' he said with a savage intensity that sent a tremor through her.

The simmering sexual tension between them was almost tangible.

Beth drew a shaky breath. 'It's the dress,' she murmured.

He gave a rough laugh. 'No, *cara*, it's you. I would

find you even more beautiful without the dress.' His eyes gleamed wickedly. 'But if you want me to prove it...'

Heat scorched her cheeks as she imagined him easing the narrow shoulder straps over her arms and then sliding the silk bodice down to reveal her naked breasts.

'Didn't you say we need to leave for the theatre at seven?' she said hurriedly.

'Before we leave there is one addition I must make to your outfit.'

From his jacket pocket he withdrew a slim velvet case, and opened it to reveal a single strand of glittering stones.

'I knew when I saw it in the jeweller's window that it would be perfect for you. It's not ostentatious or fussy— just a beautifully uncluttered design which allows the stones to shine with simple purity.'

Just as Beth's understated beauty shone from her, Cesario brooded, feeling a sharp tug of desire in his groin as he pushed her silky hair over one slender shoulder so that he could fasten the necklace around her throat.

'It's lovely.' Beth glanced in the mirror and admired the way the stones sparkled as they caught the light. 'They could almost be real diamonds.'

Cesario looked amused. 'They *are* real. What did you think—that they are glass chips?'

She gave him a horrified look. '*Real...!* It must have cost a fortune. I can't possibly accept it.'

He shrugged. 'Everyone dresses up for first-night performances at the opera house, and I'm sure you don't want to look out of place.'

Cesario could not rationalise to himself let alone to Beth why he had bought the necklace for her. There had been such sadness in her voice when she had spoken about the death of her friend Mel, and he guessed that her life in the children's home had not been happy. He enjoyed making her smile, but now she knew the diamonds were real the look of pleasure in her eyes had been replaced with wariness.

'Enjoy wearing the necklace tonight, *cara*, but do not worry that it means anything,' he advised coolly. 'It is expected that you will wear jewellery, and as you do not have any of your own I have provided you with some. That's all.'

He watched the play of emotions in her eyes: relief followed by a faint disappointment that she quickly hid beneath the sweep of her lashes.

'When you look at me like that the only place I want to take you is my bed,' he rasped.

'You shouldn't say things like that…' Beth began in an outraged tone, but the words died on her lips as he slid his hand beneath her chin and captured her mouth in a searing kiss that left her speechless.

'Why not, when it's the truth?' he taunted her softly.

But instead of kissing her again, as Beth secretly longed for him to do, he opened the door and ushered her into the hall.

'We'd better leave now, before my will-power is tested any further, *mia bella*.'

CHAPTER EIGHT

BETH was spellbound by the plush red velvet and opulent gold décor of Teatro dell'Opera. The auditorium was horse-shoe shaped, with tiers of seating boxes rising up towards a magnificent frescoed dome, and suspended from the centre of the dome was a huge chandelier of breathtaking beauty.

With her eyes focused on the ceiling, she stumbled in her high heels and felt Cesario grip her arm to steady her.

'Are you all right?' he murmured in her ear.

'Overawed,' she admitted. 'I've never been to a theatre before. This is amazing.' She glanced around at the crowd filing in to take their seats and gave him a rueful look. 'I understand now why you insisted that I should dress up. The only other people I've seen wearing so much bling are the drug dealers who trade on the estate where I live.'

He muttered something beneath his breath and slid his arm around her waist. 'Why do you live there?'

'Because it's the only place where I can afford the rent.'

'I don't want you to go back there,' Cesario said harshly. 'Even if Sophie is not my child I'll help you find some-where safer to bring her up.'

Beth could not bear the idea of him viewing her and Sophie as a charity case. 'If it turns out that she is not your responsibility why would you care what happens to her?'

He cared, Cesario realised with a frown. Little Sophie, with her button-round brown eyes and shock of dark hair, evoked a protective instinct in him. When he held her he did not consider whether or not she was his. One thing he was certain of was that, whatever the outcome of the DNA test, he would not allow Beth and the baby to return to a tower block in a crime-ridden area of East London.

They had a private box which offered a perfect view of the stage. From the moment the curtain rose Beth was transfixed by the tragic story of doomed young lovers told through the grace and beauty of ballet. But she was also desperately conscious of the man sitting beside her, she acknowledged ruefully as she darted a glance at his handsome profile. In the dark, hushed atmosphere of the theatre she was aware of the steady rise and fall of his chest, and when he moved position so that his thigh brushed against hers she felt as if an electric current had shot through her.

'Are you enjoying the performance?' Cesario asked her in the interval, when he escorted her to the bar and ordered champagne.

'This is the most magical night of my life.' Beth flushed when she realised how gauche she sounded, but nothing could diminish her pleasure in the ballet. 'I'm sorry your PA missed tonight, but thank you for inviting me.'

She stared in surprise when streaks of colour flared along his cheekbones.

'Okay, I wasn't absolutely truthful when I said I had originally planned to bring Donata,' he growled.

'What do you mean?'

'I mean that I bought the tickets for you.'

Beth's eyes widened and her heart suddenly beat faster. The bar was packed, but the sound of chattering voices and laughter, the clink of wineglasses, seemed strangely distant, and it was as if only she and Cesario existed, co-cooned in their own private world.

'Why did you do such a lovely thing?' she whispered.

'Because I hoped it would make you smile.' He held her gaze, his grey eyes gleaming with an expression that made her blood fizz. 'You have a beautiful smile, Beth Granger.'

As he watched the corners of her mouth lift in that shy smile that had such a profound effect on him Cesario felt his gut ache with desire and something else that he refused to define. He wanted to kiss her, wanted to so badly that he did not care that they were standing in a crowded bar, even though he usually abhorred making a public display. Beth had got under his skin, and at this moment he did not care who knew it. He wanted to taste her, to feel her soft lips part beneath his so that he could slide his tongue into the moist interior of her mouth.

She was watching him, waiting, and he knew from her absolute stillness that she shared his need. He bent his head, his heart hammering as he brushed his mouth across hers in a gossamer-light caress. He heard her swiftly in-drawn breath and felt an unexpected flood of tenderness mingle with the fierce hunger that corkscrewed through him.

'Cesario!'

A woman's voice sounded from close by and continued in a stream of voluble Italian. Cesario snatched his mouth from Beth's and cursed beneath his breath, before muttering, 'I'm sorry, *cara*, but you're about to meet Allegra Ricci—patron of numerous charities and the biggest gossip in Rome. There's no malice to her. She just likes to discuss everyone's business. Her husband is a good friend of mine. Fortunately for Gilberto he is hard of hearing—or at least he pretends to be when he's with his wife,' he said dryly.

He straightened and smiled coolly at the matronly woman dressed in electric-blue too-tight satin who had descended on them.

'Good evening, Allegra. Is Gilberto with you?'

'No.' She waved her hand dismissively. 'He does not enjoy the ballet so I have come with my sister.' Following Cesario's lead, Allegra Ricci now spoke in English, but she barely looked at him. Her bright black eyes were focused intently on Beth.

'And who is your delightful companion, Cesario? I don't believe we have met before.'

'This is Beth Granger.' Cesario gave the Italian woman a bland look and offered no further information, much to Allegra's obvious frustration.

'Are you staying in Rome, my dear—on holiday, perhaps?'

Faced with such a direct question, Beth felt she had no option but to reply. 'Actually I'm staying in Sardinia. At the Castello del Falco.'

Cesario checked his watch. 'We'd better make our way back to our seats. Please give my regards to Gilberto.' He nodded to Allegra and firmly led Beth away.

Her reprieve was short-lived. A visit to the cloakroom was unavoidable, and her heart sank when Allegra followed her through the door.

'So you are a guest at Cesario's home?' the Italian woman murmured. 'How intriguing. I've never known him invite any of his female friends to the castle. He usually conducts his affairs here in Rome—although it's no secret that he never keeps any of his mistresses for long.' She met Beth's eyes in the mirror and gave an unexpectedly kindly smile. 'You are so young. Forgive me for saying so, but I fear you are out of your depth with Cesario. I know he is charming, but I've heard there is a side to him that is as ruthless as his barbarian ancestors. His wife discovered that when he banished her from his castle and refused to allow her to see their baby son.'

Allegra shook her head. 'Who could blame poor Raffaella for trying to snatch Nicolo? What mother could bear to be separated from her child? Of course it was a tragedy that they were both killed. And the terrible irony for Cesario is that Raffaella and Nicolo are buried together in the grounds of the castle chapel and he is alone.'

During the second half of the performance Beth tried to concentrate on the ballet, but the magic of the evening disappeared as Allegra Ricci's insidious comments about the accident that had claimed the lives of Cesario's wife and son swirled in her mind. Why had Cesario sent Raffaella away from their little boy? Nicolo had only been two years old when he had died. A child of that age had surely needed his mother. The questions went round and round in her head, and her stomach churned with tension.

She could not bring herself to talk on the way back to his apartment. Cesario too seemed lost in his own thoughts as the limousine whisked them through the brightly lit Rome streets—still bustling with traffic even though it was nearly midnight.

Sophie hadn't stirred all evening, the nanny reported when Beth hurried straight to the nursery. 'I'll head off to bed now that you're home,' Luisa whispered.

Beth remained leaning over the cot, listening to the soft whisper of Sophie's breathing. Earlier in the day she had felt reassured by Cesario's promise that he would not separate her from Sophie if the paternity test proved she was his child. But after her conversation with Allegra Ricci she felt sick with worry. Allegra had described Cesario as ruthless. And when she pictured him at the Castello del Falco, a dark figure riding his great black horse, his falcon perched on his shoulder, a shiver ran through her. He was as uncompromising as the granite walls of his castle and she would be a fool to forget it.

She was tempted to grab Sophie and flee the apartment, but her common sense quickly reasserted itself. She was a stranger in Rome; she did not speak Italian or have money or their passports. She was trapped here, just as she had been trapped at the castle. But even if she could escape, what kind of life could she give a child in the rough area of London which was the only place she could afford to live? It would be far better for Sophie if Cesario was her father. He could give the little girl a much better life than *she* could, she acknowledged bleakly. Sophie's welfare was the only thing that mattered, Beth reminded herself. But she could not dismiss her fear that Cesario might send her away from the baby in the same way that he had apparently separated his wife from their son.

She found him in his study, a brandy glass in his hand as he stood at the window looking down at the late-night revellers who were still milling around the *piazza*. He had discarded his jacket and tie, and despite Allegra Ricci's warning that he was a ruthless womaniser Beth felt a familiar weakness in her limbs that had nothing to do with her being anaemic and everything to do with the smouldering sensuality of the man whose enigmatic expression gave no clue to his thoughts.

He turned his head when she hovered in the doorway. 'How is Sophie?'

'Asleep. Luisa says she hasn't heard a peep out of her all evening. I'm going to bed now.' For some stupid reason she blushed, and her heart-rate quickened when he strolled over to her.

'Can I get you a nightcap?' When she shook her head, he said softly, 'Did I tell you how beautiful you look to-night?'

'Several times.' She smiled, but her voice shook slightly and she caught her breath as he reached out and idly wound a lock of her long hair around his finger. The gleam in his gaze sent a tremor through her, and she closed her eyes for a moment while she sought to fight her fierce aware-ness of him.

'I came to return the necklace, but the clasp seems to be stuck.'

'Turn around and lift up your hair.'

She did as he bade, standing rigidly as his fingers brushed lightly against her neck. His warm breath whis-pered across her skin, and she trembled when he bent his head and pressed his lips to the sensitive place behind her ear. The silence was so intense that she was sure he must hear the frantic thud of her heart. She sensed he was wait-ing for a sign from her, that if she turned her head a frac-tion towards him his restraint would shatter and he would seize her in his arms and plunder her mouth with a primi-tive hunger that could only have one outcome.

Dear heaven, the temptation to give in to the molten de-sire flooding through her veins was so strong. Her heart missed a beat when he slid the strap of her dress a little way down her arm and trailed his lips over her shoulder. She knew he could see the swollen peaks of her nipples jut-ting against the clingy silk of her dress, and she imagined him peeling the material away and cupping her breasts in his hands.

She bit her lip. Was this how he had tempted Mel into his bed—with the practised ease of a skilled seducer? What would happen if she gave in to the desperate clamour of her desire? And afterwards? Would he treat her with the same callous disregard with which he had treated Mel?

She recalled Allegra Ricci's warning. *'As ruthless as his barbarian ancestors... Poor Raffaella... Banished her from his castle and refused to allow her to see their son...'*

He released the clasp and caught the necklace as it slipped from around her throat. She lowered her hands so that her hair tumbled down her back and quickly stepped away from him.

Her eyes fell on a photograph on his desk, and with a shaking hand she picked it up.

'Your son?' The resemblance to Cesario was obvious, even though the little boy in the picture was just a toddler. With a mass of unruly black curls, striking grey eyes fringed by long lashes and a happy grin, the child was enchanting.

'Yes.' Cesario's voice was suddenly terse. He drained the brandy in his glass and glanced briefly at the photo. 'That's Nicolo.'

A second photo was of Nicolo and a dark haired woman. Beth stared at her, certain from the expression of fierce adoration in the woman's eyes as she looked at the child that she was Raffaella. 'Your wife was very beautiful.'

'Yes, I suppose she was.' His indifference was chilling.

Beth swallowed, compelled to try to unlock the secrets of his past. 'You told me that you didn't love her. If that was so, why did you marry her?'

He turned his head and fixed her with a narrow stare.

As the seconds ticked by she was sure she had overstepped an invisible boundary, that she had been too intrusive and he would refuse to answer. He reached for the bottle of brandy, refilled his glass and downed half its contents in one swallow.

'It was a business arrangement—a merger between our two families, Piras and Cossu, which resulted in the formation of the largest and most successful private bank in Italy. I was brought up to believe that power is everything,' he said harshly, when he saw her shocked expression. 'Marriage to Raffaella Cossu was an opportunity that I knew would give me a level of power even my father would find impressive.' He gave a bitter laugh. 'In my arrogance I did not understand that everything comes at a price. I was taught by my father that emotions are a weakness and love is a failing—something that afflicts lesser men but never a Piras.'

Cesario took another swig of his drink and felt the burn of fiery heat at the back of his throat. He knew from experience that temporary oblivion from the demons which haunted him could be found in a bottle of spirits. There had been times since Nicolo's death when the only way he'd been able to cope with his grief had been to seek solace in alcohol. He had never revealed his pain. Not even to his closest friends. *Old habits die hard*, he thought grimly. The lessons from his childhood were deeply ingrained.

But tonight, for the first time since he was a small boy, he could not control his emotions. Something was building inside him: a need, almost a desperation to voice his feelings and release the pain that scourged his soul. It was Beth, he thought savagely. She had cast a spell on him with her slanting green eyes and made him feel things he did not want to feel. But her inherent gentleness was something he had never experienced before. He had witnessed her compassion, and he sensed that if he told her about Nicolo she would not judge him.

'Was Raffaella in love with you?' she asked softly, intuitively.

It was time to be honest and face up to the mistakes of his past. 'Perhaps,' he acknowledged heavily, 'in the early days of our marriage. But at the time I did not know it. She never spoke of her feelings, and it suited me to assume she was content with the relationship we had, based on friendship and respect. Love was an alien emotion to me—something I had been taught to deride. I did not know that I was capable of feeling it until I held my newborn son for the first time and finally understood that there is no greater power than love.'

He drained his glass and moved to the window to stare out at the crescent moon, suspended like a silver sickle against the black sky. 'I would have died for Nicolo,' he said roughly. 'He was my purpose in life, my reason for being, and nothing else mattered—not power or wealth, not the bank. I loved my boy beyond reason. What I failed to understand was that Raffaella loved Nicolo just as deeply.'

'Allegra Ricci said that you sent Raffaella away and refused to allow her to see Nicolo.'

'That's not true. Raffaella had an affair and wanted to leave me for her lover. I can't blame her. I couldn't give her the marriage she wanted or deserved,' Cesario admitted grimly. 'But I couldn't let her take our son. The idea of living apart from him, of being sidelined in his life while another man took on the role of father to him, tore me apart. I was willing to share custody. I had been separated from my own mother at a young age, and I considered it vital that Nicolo spent an equal amount of time with his mother as with me. However, I felt it was better for his main home to be the Castello del Falco. Raffaella didn't agree, and was desperate for him to live with her. Our relationship disintegrated and the rows grew more acrimonious.'

Cesario's voice rasped in his throat. 'After a particularly bad confrontation Raffaella snatched Nicolo and fled with him. It had been raining, and she probably drove too fast.' He delivered the words in a tightly controlled monotone. 'I heard the crash—it's a sound that still haunts my dreams. I guessed what had happened. As I ran, I prayed I was wrong. But my worst fears became a nightmare when I saw that the car had skidded off the road and ploughed down the side of the mountain.'

He heard Beth draw a sharp breath, but now that he had opened the floodgates the words kept on coming in an unstoppable tide. 'I managed to climb down, hanging onto rocks, tree roots. The car had flipped over and landed on its roof. I saw instantly that Raffaella was dead, but Nicolo…I prayed he was still alive.'

'Dear God,' Beth whispered. She wanted to walk over to Cesario and take his hand, offer him what comfort she could. But something told her he needed to relive his agonising memories, that this was perhaps the first time since the accident that he had talked about what had happened that day.

'I had to smash the window with my bare hands to get him out. I didn't even feel the broken glass slice open my face.' He ran his hand over his scar and his voice dropped to a harsh whisper, as if his throat had been scraped raw with sandpaper. 'I was like a madman. I was frantic to save my boy, to hold him in my arms and see his smile, to hear him call me *Papà*. But he had gone.' His voice shook. 'My son was dead.'

Tears were running down Beth's cheeks, but she brushed them away as she flew across the room and halted in front of Cesario. It tore her heart to see his hard-boned face ravaged with pain. How could she have believed him to be unemotional? She knew now that his way of dealing with the devastation of losing his son had been to bury his emotions deep inside him. But tonight his agony was raw and exposed, and impelled by a desire to try to comfort him she slipped her arms around his waist and held him tightly, willing him to believe that she understood his grief.

For a moment he stiffened, but then he put his arms around her and held her, and Beth felt some of the terrible tension that gripped him slowly ease.

'The accident was my fault,' he said roughly.

'No! How can you say that? Raffaella—'

'Raffaella was torn between her feelings for the man she had fallen in love with and her love for her son. For Nicolo's sake I should have tried harder to reach an agreement with her on how we could share his upbringing, instead of forcing her into a desperate act that had such tragic consequences.'

He stepped away from her and walked over to the desk to pour another glass of brandy before sinking onto the sofa. He tugged her down beside him, curving an arm around her shoulders as if he needed the physical contact.

'The party to celebrate the opening of the English subsidiary of the Piras-Cossu Bank in London last year was on the anniversary of the date Nicolo died. I didn't want to go, but I had a duty to attend.' Cesario swirled the amber liquid around in his glass. 'It wasn't the first time I'd turned to alcohol to numb my mind. God knows how much I drank that night.' He grimaced. 'It shames me to admit I have no memory of Melanie Stewart. The DNA test will prove if I slept with her. If it is true, then I cannot condone my behaviour and I regret that I clearly did not treat her with consideration and respect.'

'I don't think anyone could blame you for drinking too much when you were grieving for your little boy,' Beth said gently. 'Sometimes the only way to cope with painful memories is to try to block them out.' She swallowed the lump in her throat. 'I think Mel would have understood.' Just as *she* understood, she thought with fierce compassion. Cesario hadn't behaved with deliberate disregard for Mel. He had been suffering that night in London, tortured with grief for the son he had adored.

Her heart clenched when she saw the betraying dampness on his eyelashes. It hurt her to see this formidable, strong man suddenly so vulnerable, and she felt guilty that she was intruding on his privacy. 'I'll go,' she whispered. 'I'm sure you must want to be alone.'

Cesario looked into Beth's soft green eyes and felt the hard knot in his chest loosen a little. He had been alone for the past four years and had mourned his son the only way he knew how—by ignoring his pain and never revealing his emotions. He couldn't explain why he had opened up to a woman he barely knew, but in a strange way he felt he had known Beth for ever, and he trusted her more than he had ever trusted another human being.

Dio! Where had that thought come from? he wondered.

Her silky hair felt soft against his cheek and smelled of lemons. He closed his eyes and inhaled deeply. He could still taste the acrid burn of tears in his throat, but talking about Nicolo had given him a curious sense of release.

He pulled Beth closer. 'Stay a while?' he said gruffly.

And a sense of peace settled over him as she rested her head on his shoulder and they sat in silence, sharing an empathy that went deeper than words.

Cesario had returned to the castle. Beth heard the sound of the helicopter as she watched the first pink streaks of dawn spread across the sky. Her heart lifted at the prospect of seeing him again, but she also felt apprehensive.

It was three days since she had woken at the apartment in Rome and discovered that she had slept in the red evening dress she had worn to the ballet. She'd realised she must have fallen asleep on the sofa in Cesario's study and he had carried her to her room. The maid had informed her that he had already gone to the Piras-Cossu Bank, and that he had arranged for her to fly back to the Castello del Falco with Sophie and Luisa Moretti.

She'd wondered if he had been deliberately avoiding her—if perhaps he regretted revealing his emotions to her. After all, he had been brought up to hide his feelings, and had been taught by his father that for Piras men, emotions were a sign of weakness.

Too restless to remain in bed, she jumped up and pulled open her wardrobe. The new clothes she had discovered hanging there when she had returned from Rome were definitely something she would bring up with Cesario. The red dress had been necessary for her to wear to the theatre, but she could not accept all these beautiful designer outfits, she thought wistfully as she ran her hand over the silk and satin and softest cashmere, in pretty rainbow colours that were such a contrast to the dull clothes she had brought to Sardinia.

For now, she *had* to choose something from the extensive selection. Her own clothes had disappeared and the maid Carlotta looked blank every time Beth asked her what had happened to them. Taking a pale blue wrap-around dress from its hanger, she walked into the bathroom and emerged fifteen minutes later, having showered and dressed and blasted her hair with the drier.

Sophie had fed at 5:00 a.m. and would sleep soundly for several hours. The early-morning sunshine beckoned as Beth crept out of the nursery and walked quickly through the silent castle, crossing the entrance hall to the front door that opened onto the courtyard.

The sky was a clear forget-me-not blue, promising another warm spring day, although the mountain peaks on the horizon were hidden by clouds. Beth had intended to sit in the gardens at the rear of the castle, but the sound of horse's hooves on cobblestones made her glance over her shoulder, and her breath snagged in her throat when she saw Cesario riding across the courtyard.

Dressed entirely in black, his long, tousled hair gleaming like a raven's wing in the sunlight, he looked as she imagined his medieval ancestors must have done—especially with his falcon, Gratia, perched on his shoulder. His hard-boned face was inscrutable, and the scar running down his cheek pulled at the corner of his eye, giving him a narrowed gaze that hid his thoughts.

He halted in front of her, and she wondered despairingly if she would ever break free from the spell he had cast on her. 'You're back,' she greeted him, flushing when she realised the inanity of the statement. 'I meant…I didn't know how long you would be in Rome.'

Cesario took pity on her, intrigued that she had clearly felt the same rush of pleasure that had swept like wildfire through his veins when he had caught sight of her poised like a slender wraith on the castle steps.

'Thanks to technology I am able to work mainly from the castle, but it was necessary for me to stay in the city for the last couple of days to deal with matters that required my personal attention.' He studied her speculatively. 'I've just been up to the chapel. I'm guessing it was you who put flowers on Nicolo's grave?'

'Yes. I hope you don't mind that I put them on Raffaella's too?' She looked at him uncertainly. 'I can't help but feel sad for her. She died so young and in such tragic circumstances.'

'Why should I mind?' he said quietly. 'I know all about your soft heart, Beth Granger. I hear that in my absence your stray dog has made himself at home in the castle and follows you around like a faithful shadow.'

Despite his stern tone, Cesario did not seem annoyed. There was something different about him, Beth mused. He seemed more relaxed and at peace with himself. He smiled, causing her heart to miss a beat. It was the first time she had seen him smile with his eyes as well as his mouth, and the frank sensuality in his gaze filled her with a yearning so intense that it felt like a clawing sensation in the pit of her stomach.

'Come with me?' he said, stretching his hand down to her. 'There is no place more beautiful in the world than the mountains on a clear morning.'

'I'm not dressed for riding,' she whispered, catching her breath when he lifted her effortlessly and placed her on the saddle in front of him.

'Perhaps not, but you look very beautiful, *cara mia*. The dress suits you.'

Beth found it hard to think of anything but the feel of his big, hard body pressed up against hers as they rode out of the courtyard—but she could not allow herself to be overwhelmed by him, she told herself firmly.

'About the clothes that have magically appeared in my wardrobe—I can't allow you to pay for them so I'm afraid you must send them back.'

'Well, I certainly have no objection to you walking around the castle naked,' he murmured, lowering his head so that his warm breath tickled her ear.

Heat flooded through her, and the sweet, urgent throb in her pelvis grew more insistent. 'Of course I won't be naked. I'll wear my own clothes.'

'Ah—that could be difficult, since I asked the gardener to burn them.'

She half twisted round on the saddle so that she could glare at him. 'Why on earth did you do that?'

'Because you are too exquisite to dress like a drab sparrow.' He smiled at her startled expression. 'Now, stop arguing and tell me what you think of the view.'

His horse had carried them along a winding path up the mountainside, and now they had reached a flat grassy plateau bordered by a crystal clear stream that babbled and chattered over the rocks. The falcon had been sitting patiently on his shoulder, but at his command she spread her wings and rose into the air with incredible grace and speed. Within seconds she was a speck high in the sky.

'It's incredible,' Beth murmured, turning her head to scan the panoramic view of the mountains, whose pale limestone peaks emerged from the lush green woodland which covered their lower slopes. Far below was the town of Oliena, with its square white-brick houses looking like toy building blocks and their terracotta roofs glinting in the sunshine.

Cesario dismounted and lifted her down from the sad-

dle. 'I feel closest to Nicolo here,' he admitted. He spread
a rug on the ground and invited her to sit beside him. 'He
would be six years old now. I imagine him riding up here
with me on his own pony, or kicking a football around the
castle courtyard.' He stared into the distance, seemingly
lost in his thoughts, but then he turned to her.

'Since we spoke the other night I've been thinking about
my son, and for the first time since the accident I've been
able to look at photographs of him and remember him with
joy. The sadness is still there,' he said huskily. 'I'll always
miss him. But I have so many happy memories of him and
I don't want to push them away any more. I want to share
them.'

Instinctively Beth placed her hand over his. 'Tell me
about Nicolo,' she said softly.

She lost track of time as they talked. He recounted tender memories of Nicolo, and at his prompting she told him
about Sophie's premature birth and her anxious vigil while
the baby had been in the special care unit. She revealed her
pain and shock at Mel's death, and spoke of their friendship which had started at the children's home.

A cool breeze ruffling her hair reminded her of where
they were, and she glanced around, startled to see that the
sun had disappeared behind dark clouds.

'Do you think it's going to rain?'

'Undoubtedly.' Cesario looked behind him to the mountain peaks, and Beth gasped as she followed his gaze and
saw an ominous black mass rolling across the sky. A thun-
derclap as loud as cannon-fire made her flinch and then
the heavens opened: raindrops the size of pennies falling
with such ferocity that they were soaked within seconds.

'Come.' He lifted her onto the horse and swung up onto
the saddle behind her.

'What about Gratia?' Beth asked anxiously.

As she spoke, Cesario blew on a whistle, and moments later the bird of prey flew down and landed on his shoulder.

He urged his horse forward, but instead of heading down the path he took them higher, skirting the forest until they came to a clearing where a wooden cabin stood, half hidden among the trees.

'Get inside.' He had to shout to be heard above the torrential rain, but Beth—drenched and shivering—needed no second bidding, and ran for shelter while he took the horse and the falcon into the adjoining stable.

The cabin was basic—just one main room housing a cooking stove, a table and a couple of chairs, and in the far corner an old-fashioned wrought-iron bedstead. Efforts had been made to give the place a homely feel, with brightly coloured rugs on the floor and crisp white cotton sheets on the bed.

'*Dio*, what a deluge.' Cesario followed her inside, shaking his wet hair out of his eyes.

He disappeared through a door, returning moments later to throw her a towel. He had already stripped off his shirt, and Beth's eyes were drawn to the beads of moisture clinging to his dark chest hairs. He frowned when she made no attempt to dry herself. Water was dripping from her dress and her teeth were chattering.

'Come, *cara*, you need to get out of your wet clothes.' He strode over to her, his hands reaching for the belt that secured her dress, and began to tug the knot loose.

'Don't…' she said jerkily. The abrupt transition from warm sunshine to freezing rain had been such a shock to her body that she was shivering violently and could barely speak. She tried to push his hands away, but he ignored her and untied the belt. Desperate to halt him, she muttered, 'I'm not wearing…' Her words faded as he pushed the edges of the dress apart and released his breath in a slow hiss. 'A bra…'

'So I see.' Eyes locked on her body, he peeled the wet fabric from her shoulders and allowed the dress to fall at her feet. *'Santa Madonna,'* he said harshly. 'You are exquisite.'

CHAPTER NINE

THE primitive hunger in Cesario's voice sent a tremor through Beth. The rain was hammering down on the roof of the cabin, but the prickling silence between them was so profound that she was sure he could hear the erratic thud of her heart. He lifted his hand and very lightly traced her collarbone, and then slowly, delicately, almost as if he was afraid she would break, he skimmed his fingers down to her breast.

She caught her breath as he explored the small rounded contour, his tanned fingers contrasting starkly with her creamy flesh. His eyes were hooded but she glimpsed the feral gleam beneath his heavy lids and could not restrain a little gasp when he stroked her nipple. It tautened instantly at his touch, and the sensation of his fingers gently squeezing her tender flesh was so acute that a quiver of intense heat shot from her breast to her pelvis.

'*Sei bella*, Beth,' he growled in a thick, sexually charged tone that caressed her senses like the sumptuous feel of velvet against her skin. With his free hand he cupped her other breast and she made a little choked sound when he rolled its dusky peak between his thumb and forefinger.

'I want you.' His voice cracked. '*Dio mio*, you are like a fever in my blood. And you want me too. Your body does not lie, *cara*,' he said fiercely. 'The attraction burned between us from the moment we first met and neither of us can ignore it any longer.'

It was true, Beth acknowledged helplessly. She had felt an intense awareness, an inexplicable connection with him when she had first seen him on the night she had arrived at the castle. She remembered she had felt a curious sensation, like an arrow piercing her heart, and she felt it again now. But now she knew what it was.

Love, she thought shakily. She had looked into Cesario's granite grey eyes and she had been lost for ever.

Of course she had denied it to herself. Love at first sight only happened in fairy tales, and Cesario was no Prince Charming; he was a heartless playboy who had been too drunk to remember sleeping with Mel. She had told herself she despised him, but as she had learned more about his past her heart had softened and she had understood how his grief for his son had caused him to behave in a way that he regretted.

'Beth?'

He said her name raggedly, as if he feared her silence meant he had been mistaken to think she shared his desire. She saw the tension in his jaw and lifted a trembling hand to his face, gently tracing the livid scar down to the corner of his mouth.

'Was I wrong to think, to hope, that the fire inside me burns in you too?'

'No,' she whispered, 'you weren't wrong.' And, standing on tiptoe, she reached up and kissed him.

With a savage groan he wrapped his arms around her and pulled her hard against him, so that the tips of her breasts brushed the wiry hairs that covered his broad chest. The sensation was so exquisitely erotic that she gasped;

the sound was muffled by his lips as he slanted his mouth over hers and kissed her with a feverish hunger that warned her there could be no going back. He meant to possess her, and she welcomed his passionate urgency, parting her lips so that he could thrust his tongue between them to explore the moistness within.

She snatched a breath when at last he lifted his mouth from hers and trailed a line of kisses down her throat, to capture the pulse jerking erratically at its base. His hands caressed her breasts once more, and then, to her startled delight, he lowered his head and closed his lips around one nipple to suckle the rosy peak until the pleasure was almost unbearable.

She moaned softly and clung to him while he transferred his attention to her other nipple, lashing it with his tongue until it was pebble-hard. She shivered—not with cold, but with a heated desire that was growing ever more frantic. Molten warmth pooled between her thighs and she ached there, ached for him to touch her and give her the sweet release her body craved.

The room tilted as Cesario swept her into his arms and carried her over to the bed. He laid her down on the cool sheets and held her gaze as he hooked his fingers into the waistband of her knickers.

There was something incredibly sexy about Beth's simple plain cotton underwear, Cesario brooded. His already hardened shaft strained uncomfortably against his trousers as he pulled her knickers down to reveal the neat triangle of curls that hid her femininity.

He wanted her to undress him, for her to stroke his throbbing length with her soft white hands. But the mere thought of her caressing him brought him to the edge of no return, and with more haste than grace he stripped and lowered himself onto the bed.

Her hair felt like silk. He ran his fingers through its length and then cupped her face, bringing his mouth down on hers once more in a sensual kiss, seeking a response that she gave with such sweet eagerness that his heart clenched.

But although she kissed him with a fervour that made him ache she seemed curiously shy, and did not boldly explore his body as an experienced mistress would do. He sensed her faint wariness, and instinct warned him she had not had many other lovers.

His jaw tensed when he recalled her telling him how her ex-employer had assaulted her. No wonder she seemed tentative. There was a need for restraint, for him to slow the pace and arouse her with gentle care. It would take all his will-power, he acknowledged ruefully. He could not remember ever being so turned on. But from the outset Beth had cast a spell on him with her slanting green eyes and he was utterly lost to her magic.

Beth's heart thudded when Cesario trailed his hands slowly down her body. He seemed in no rush, and the realisation that he was controlling his urgent desire helped her to relax. The unpleasant memories of Hugo Devington's clumsy attempts to touch her body faded from her mind. She trusted Cesario completely. He treated her as his equal and she knew he would make love to her with consideration and respect.

Excitement fluttered inside her when he skimmed his fingertips lightly over her stomach and traced the indent of her waist, before moving lower to carefully ease her legs apart. It was new and wondrous, and she held her breath as he brushed his fingers in a gossamer-soft caress up and down her moist opening. She felt no shyness, just a fierce need that made her spread her legs wider and lift her hips as he parted her and slid an exploratory finger between her slick folds.

Slowly her internal muscles relaxed, allowing him to push deeper, and she gave a startled cry of pleasure when he bent his head to her breast and laved one nipple and then its twin with his tongue while he continued his erotic exploration of her body with his fingers.

Reality faded and she entered an almost dream-like state dominated by the incredible sensations Cesario was arousing in her. She curled her hands into the sheet, her whole being focused on the rhythmic pulse of his finger slipping in and out of her and the delicate brush of his thumb pad across the ultra-sensitive nub of her clitoris.

'Touch me, *cara*,' he said roughly.

She opened her eyes and her heart lurched when she saw the feral hunger in his gaze. He took her hand and guided her down to his solid length. Steel encased in velvet, she thought wonderingly, and so big—surely he was too big for her to take him inside her?

She felt a flutter of apprehension, but at the same time her body ached for something more than the delicate caress of his hands. A fierce need was building inside her—a need that she sensed would only be assuaged when he replaced his finger with the hard arousal that was already pushing between her thighs.

He kissed her mouth, deep and slow, and the inherent tenderness of the kiss dismissed her faint fear. She trusted him, and her tense muscles relaxed, so that when he slid his hands beneath her bottom and lifted her she bent her knees and opened for him, her heart-rate quickening as the tip of him pressed against her welcoming moisture.

He groaned, but instead of pushing forward he withdrew and rested his brow lightly on hers, his chest heaving as he fought for control. 'I must protect you, *cara*,' he muttered, lifting himself from her. 'Don't go away.'

Mystified, she watched him stride through a door which she saw led into the tiny bathroom. Why was he leaving her? Had he decided not to make love to her? Her body throbbed with unfulfilled desire. But he was back within seconds, pausing to slide a rubber sheath over his burgeoning manhood before he knelt over her and sank between her spread thighs.

'*Carissima*,' he whispered, and surged forward—only to halt again when he felt the fragile barrier of her virginity. 'Beth?' He stared into her wide eyes, stunned to see the faint trepidation in their green depths. 'Your first time?'

There was no point in lying. 'Yes.' She felt him pull back and frantically gripped his shoulders. 'Are you going to stop?'

'Do you want me to?' he asked hoarsely.

She shook her head, and driven by innate honesty admitted, 'I want you to be the first.'

Cesario expelled his breath on a ragged sigh. She was so lovely, his English rose. And now she would be truly his.

'If I had known I would have taken things more slowly,' he murmured, bending his head to anoint each of her reddened nipples with his lips. He heard her soft gasp, and with great care he slowly eased forward. He felt the initial restraint of her body and slanted his mouth over hers to catch her faint surprised cry as he pushed through the delicate membrane and surged deep into her.

He fitted perfectly, Beth thought, a sweet languor stealing over as the stinging pain of his possession quickly passed. He filled her, completed her, and she arched her hips to welcome each thrust of his rigid length, discovering as she did so that he was taking her on a journey of such intense pleasure that she hoped it would never end. Urgency replaced her languor, and she twisted her head on the pillow as he drove into her with long, measured strokes, setting a rhythm that took her quickly to the edge of some unknown place and held her there, gasping and sobbing his name, as the first spasms rippled from her central core.

Beads of sweat glistened on his bronzed shoulders and she sensed instinctively that he was fighting to control the insistent demands of his body. His skin was drawn taut over his razor-sharp cheekbones and his eyes glittered with a primitive hunger that sent a thrill of excitement through her. He thrust again, the deepest yet, and she shattered, her slender body arching as spasm after spasm ripped through her in an unending tide of indescribable pleasure.

He gripped her hips and held her tight, increased his pace, faster, harder, while she convulsed around him until with a groan rent from deep in his soul he reached his own release and buried his face in her fragrant hair as his seed pumped from him.

It was a long time before Cesario lifted his head from where he had pillowed it on her breasts. The ragged sound of their breathing had gradually slowed, and Beth became aware that the rain had eased to a soft pitter-patter on the roof of the cabin.

Tension seeped into her when he propped himself on his elbows and stared into her eyes, his hard-boned face as enigmatic as ever. She did not know what he expected. Should she make a witty remark or compliment him on his performance? What was the protocol between two people who had indulged in casual sex? she wondered bleakly.

Her heart leapt with relief when he smiled softly and bent his head to claim her mouth in a tender kiss. 'So that was your first lesson in making love, *mia bella*.' He laughed ruefully at her shocked expression when she felt the unmistakable sign that he was already aroused again, his hardened shaft pushing against her hip. 'As you can feel, I am an impatient tutor, and my body is eager to give you your second lesson.'

'Why don't you, then?' she invited daringly, feeling a flood of silken heat between her legs.

To her disappointment he eased away from her and stood up. 'Because I must be patient and allow your body time to recover from any soreness.' He could not resist dropping another kiss on the slight pout of her lips. 'We have plenty of time, *cara*,' he assured her gently.

Beth did not like to think of time. The results of the DNA test would be known in a matter of days, and if they proved that Cesario was not Sophie's father she would take the baby back to England and probably never see him again. He had proved how much he desired her, but she was under no illusion that he wanted anything more than a brief affair with her.

Feeling agitated, she swung her legs over the side of the bed and to her horror saw a small, betraying bloodstain on the sheet. Cesario returned from the bathroom and she flushed when his eyes settled briefly on the mark.

'I'm sorry. I'll change the sheet...' A host of confused emotions surged up inside her, and inexplicably she burst into tears.

'Shh, *carissima*.' Cesario swept her into his arms, feeling a curious tug on his heart at the sight of her distress. 'The sheet is not important. Come.' He carried her into the bathroom where the bath was filling, and lowered her into the fragrant bubbles.

Beth let out a shaky sigh as she sank into the warm water and felt the tension seep from her body. 'I don't know why I'm being so silly.' She was embarrassed by her tears and quickly rubbed her hand over her face.

'Not silly,' he assured her in his deep, velvet-soft voice. 'Just very lovely, and rather more innocent that I had expected,' he added wryly.

He knew he should feel guilty that he had taken her virginity, but he could not regret the most profoundly moving experience of his life, Cesario thought fiercely. He felt a sense of honour that she had chosen him and another curious sensation—a golden glow inside him that he hadn't felt for a long time but which he realised with surprise was happiness.

'I can manage,' Beth protested when Cesario tipped shampoo into his palm.

His eyes met hers and his gentle smile made her heart ache with a longing that he… She caught her lip between her teeth and told herself to be sensible. Just because he had made love to her so beautifully it did not mean that he loved her. But when he looked at her as he was doing now, she couldn't help but believe that he cared for her a little.

'Humour me, hmm…?' he murmured, and proceeded to wash and rinse her hair before he lifted her out of the bath and wrapped a towel around her.

It was a novel experience to be taken care of, and Beth gave herself up to the tender ministrations of his hands as he dried her and carried her back to the bed. He stretched out beside her and kissed her, parting her lips and tasting her with little sips that deepened to something innately sensual.

Her skin was like satin, Cesario thought as he explored her with his mouth, sucking gently on each of her swollen nipples before moving lower to ease her legs apart and bestow the most intimate caress of all. She gave a little gasp, shock quickly turning to delight, and he smiled and set about his self-appointed task, using his tongue and all his skill and patience until she writhed and sobbed his name, and he tasted her feminine fragrance as she climaxed beneath him.

'Sleep for a while,' he murmured when he took her back in his arms and brushed his lips across her hair.

She looked at him uncertainly. 'But don't you want to…?'

'That was for you, *cara*.' He ruthlessly controlled his throbbing need and watched her eyelashes flutter against her cheeks.

There was plenty of time for him to make love to her fully and experience the pleasure of their mutual satisfaction, Cesario mused as he settled her head on his shoulder. Whatever the outcome of the DNA test, he saw no reason why Beth should not remain at the castle as his mistress. Not for ever, of course. He did not *do* for ever.

He frowned, wondering why the prospect of ending their relationship—as he surely would eventually—was such an unwelcome thought. But he could not imagine his desire for her fading any time soon. He had been captivated by a green-eyed witch and he was in no rush to escape her magic.

'I'm sure Sophie has gained a few pounds,' Beth remarked as she cuddled the baby before handing her to Cesario.

'Luisa has a set of baby scales and she's going to weigh her later.'

They were in the castle gardens, enjoying the spring sunshine that shone from an azure sky, although Sophie—who had been propped up on a pile of cushions on the rug—was protected from the sun by a parasol which provided plenty of shade.

Cesario settled the little girl in the crook of his arm and covered her dark hair with a sunhat before he strolled over to one of the ornamental pools so that she could watch the fountain splashing into the water.

'I wouldn't be surprised if you've put on a couple of pounds too,' he murmured, when Beth walked over to join him. His gaze dropped to her low-cut strap-top. 'Not that I have any complaints, *cara*. Your breasts are definitely fuller. How do you expect me to do any work when you're such a sexy distraction?'

She laughed and pushed her silky brown hair over her shoulders, her eyes glowing in a face that was no longer pale and drawn but as tanned as the rest of her slim body. A combination of iron tablets and good food meant that she was no longer anaemic. She still did not get much sleep at night, but she could not blame Sophie. The baby now slept through the night, and if she did stir, the nanny, Luisa, now occupied the bedroom adjoining the nursery and was on hand to see to her.

No, her sleepless nights were for a very different reason, Beth mused, feeling the familiar lurch of her heart when Cesario gave her a sultry smile that had the immediate effect of making her blood zing in her veins.

'Considering how many times we made love last night, I would have thought you would be glad of a few hours shut away in your study while you restore your energy.'

'I am fully recuperated,' he assured her dryly, his eyes glinting with amusement and possessive heat. 'A fact that I intend to prove while Sophie has her afternoon nap.'

He chuckled when Beth blushed furiously. 'I can't imagine what the staff must think about the amount of time we spend in bed,' she muttered.

'You know all the staff are charmed by you. Even Teodoro smiles when your name is mentioned, and several times I've caught him feeding your ugly dog titbits from the kitchen.'

'Harry's not ugly—he's adorable. Aren't you?' she said, bending down to stroke the ever-faithful scruffy dog who looked up at her with adoration in his soulful brown eyes.

Was it crazy to feel jealous of the attention Beth lavished on a mutt? Cesario asked himself impatiently. He contented himself with the knowledge that soon he would sweep her upstairs to the master bedroom and lay her down on his huge four-poster bed. He would remove her clothes and she would strip him and run her soft hands over his chest and thighs, before closing her fingers around his swollen shaft.

He glanced down at Sophie and saw she had fallen asleep in his arms. Her long dark lashes curled on her pink cheeks. She was as pretty as a doll, and he felt a gentle tug on his heart as he carried her into the castle and handed her to the nanny. Any day now they should hear back from the clinic. Was it crazy to hope that Sophie *was* his daughter? Cesario wondered. The circumstances surrounding her conception were not ideal. He still found it hard to believe that, in a drunken state, he'd had sex with a woman he had no recollection of, but he had to accept the possibility that he had slept with Melanie Stewart. If Sophie was his, he would have no regrets about her birth.

'I think we should follow Sophie's lead and take a siesta,' he told Beth as he scooped her up and strode towards the stairs.

She wound her arms around his neck and appeared to consider his suggestion. 'I suppose we could. Or you could give me another riding lesson. Or we could visit the falconry. Or sit in the library and read about the history of the castle and your, I have to say, rather bloodthirsty ancestors.'

Cesario silently reflected on the past two weeks which, if he was honest with himself, had been the happiest time he'd known in the four years since he had lost his son. And it was all down to the woman in his arms.

'No wonder I get so little work done when I prefer to spend all my time with you.' He paused on the landing and kissed her with fierce passion, until reality faded and she clung to him, her body pliant and desperate for his possession.

'I wish you didn't have to go away later today. Four days is a long time and I'm going to miss you.' Beth sighed, uncaring that she might be giving too much away. They had barely spent any time apart since they had become lovers, and she hated the prospect of four long days and even longer nights without Cesario.

'I'm afraid my trip to Japan is unavoidable, *cara*.' He hesitated, and then said gruffly, 'I'll miss you too.'

How had she slipped into his life without him realising how important she had become to him? he wondered. He wasn't looking forward to his business trip because it meant four nights when she would not fall asleep in his arms, and he would wake in the mornings to an empty bed rather than to her smile.

'I may be able to wrap things up quickly and come home

early. And I don't have to leave yet. What would you like to do for the next hour, *mia bella*?'

'I would like you to make love to me, please,' she told him, in an innocent voice that did not match the wicked gleam in her eyes.

Cesario laughed out loud, and then halted abruptly and gave her an intent look. 'The castle isn't used to the sound of laughter. It was a rare occurrence when I was growing up here, and since Nicolo died this has been a place of sadness.'

'There wasn't a lot of laughter in my childhood, either,' Beth admitted. 'I never knew I could feel like this—' She broke off, afraid he would guess how she felt about him. But it wasn't in her nature to be secretive. 'You make me happy,' she whispered.

Cesario wanted to tell her that she made him happy too, but the lessons of his childhood were deeply ingrained. He had never in his life told anyone how he felt. He was not good at expressing his emotions verbally, he acknowledged. But every time he made love to her he showed her with tender caresses of his hands and mouth that she had crept under his guard, and he could not imagine a time when he would want to let her go.

His mobile rang as he strode into the bedroom and deposited Beth on the bed. He felt a pang of guilt for his PA as he went to switch off the phone. Donata had spent the past couple of weeks postponing his appointments and making excuses for why he was unavailable. But when he glanced at the caller display he saw that it was not his secretary, and his heart lurched.

'I'm sorry, *cara*, I need to take this.'

'I have to pop to the bathroom.' Beth slid off the bed

and Cesario waited until she had closed the door of the *en-suite* before answering the call.

The bedroom was empty when she re-emerged. Beth assumed his call had been about work and he had gone down to his study. But then she heard voices from the baby monitor—Cesario speaking in a low tone to the nanny. Thinking that Sophie must be awake, she hurried along the corridor and met Luisa coming out of the nursery.

'Is something wrong? Was Sophie crying?'

'Oh, no, she's fast asleep,' Luisa assured her.

Puzzled, Beth opened the nursery door. Cesario was standing by the cot, looking down at Sophie with a curious expression on his face. Feeling an inexplicable sense of foreboding, she walked quietly into the room.

He glanced at her and moved over to the window, motioning her to join him there.

'The phone call was from the DNA testing clinic,' he said without preamble. 'I am not Sophie's father.'

'Not…!' A host of emotions hit Beth—shock, faint relief that Cesario had no claim to Sophie, followed immediately by disappointment for the baby, whose future would be dictated by this momentous news. Sophie would not now enjoy the comfortable upbringing that being the daughter of a billionaire would have assured her. And more importantly she would never know the identity of her father. She had no daddy to love and protect her, Beth thought sadly. And with her mother dead Sophie was desperately vulnerable and utterly dependent on *her*.

As the implication of the news sank in she stared anxiously at Cesario. 'Mel must have been mistaken. Unless…' A terrible doubt crept into her mind as she thought back to that day in the hospital when Mel had told her she had recognised a photo in the newspaper of the man she had slept with months before.

'*The paper says he is Cesario Piras, billionaire owner of the Piras-Cossu Bank. He is Sophie's father and she has a right to a huge maintenance allowance from him.*'

Surely Mel couldn't have made up the story that she had slept with Cesario? It wouldn't have made sense for her to lie when a DNA test could prove paternity. But what if Mel hadn't considered a DNA test? What if, seriously ill, perhaps even sensing that she did not have long to live, she had seen the picture of Cesario, remembered that he had been drinking heavily at the party, and guessed he wouldn't remember anything of that night?

'Unless what?' Cesario demanded.

Beth's mind reeled. Had Mel taken a desperate gamble to try and arrange financial security for her baby daughter by dishonestly claiming that Cesario was the father of her child? If so, it meant she had knowingly involved Beth in what amounted to a scam, with the intention of getting money from him.

No wonder he looked so grim, she thought sickly. From the coldness in his granite-grey gaze he clearly believed that Mel had lied, and that *she* had been part of the subterfuge.

'Unless what?' he said again.

His hooded gaze hid his thoughts, but Beth sensed he was angry.

'Nothing,' she whispered. 'It's obviously all been a huge mistake.'

She could not bear the hard look in his eyes when only a few minutes ago—before he'd had the call from the clinic—he had looked at her as if…as if he cared for her a little. She swallowed. Stupid thought. Of course he didn't care for her; he simply enjoyed having sex with her. But now there was no reason for her to remain at the castle. Their affair would end, she would take Sophie back to East London, and within a short time Cesario would no doubt forget that either of them existed.

'I don't believe Mel lied,' she said fiercely. 'She was my best friend and we were always honest with each other. I don't understand why she was so sure you were the father of her baby.'

He shrugged. 'I've always found it difficult to believe that I could have spent the night with a woman and have no memory at all of her. Now I know I didn't sleep with Melanie Stewart. The results are indisputable. They show probability of my paternity to be nought percent—meaning it is one hundred percent certain that Sophie is not my child.'

The words settled like lead weights in Cesario's chest. He did not have a daughter. The angelic little girl who was sleeping peacefully in the cot, blissfully unaware of the furore surrounding her, was not his.

He walked back across the room and stared down at Sophie. Beth was right; she had grown in the past two weeks. She was lying with her arms outstretched, the tiny fingers on one hand curled around the silk ribbon attached to her favourite teddy. Her pink cheeks were petal soft and her mass of dark hair still reminded him of Nicolo, even though he now knew that any resemblance between her and his son had been purely in his imagination.

Dio, he hadn't expected to feel so gutted that she wasn't his, he thought painfully. Sweet little Sophie, with her button-round eyes and gummy smile, was adorable. Only a person with a heart of stone could not love her—and he had discovered recently that his heart had the consistency of a marshmallow, he acknowledged derisively.

How vulnerable she was, this tiny child who would never know her real father or mother. She had a guardian, of course. He knew Beth loved Sophie. But Beth lived in a run-down tower block in a part of London where crime and drug dealing were rife. It was no place to bring up a child.

He could not allow them to go back there, Cesario thought adamantly. Sophie had slipped into his heart and helped ease the pain of losing his son. He wanted to protect her—and Beth too, he admitted. He hated the thought of her scraping a living and struggling to bring up her friend's child on her own.

He would give her money, he brooded. He would set up a fund for Sophie and buy a house in England so that Beth could care for the baby in pleasant and safe surroundings. Although, knowing her stubborn pride, he would have his work cut out to persuade her to accept financial help from him, he thought ruefully.

There was no need for him to do more than offer his assistance. The child and her guardian were not his responsibility. So why did he hate the thought of Beth and Sophie leaving the castle? Why did he feel, Cesario thought savagely, that his heart had been torn from his chest and the happiness he'd felt these past few weeks was trickling away as fast as sand in an egg-timer?

CHAPTER TEN

AN HOUR later, Cesario found Beth in the master bedroom that they had shared since they had become lovers. She did not glance at him as he walked into the room, but continued to fold items of clothing and place them in her suitcase.

'What are you doing?'

'Packing, of course.' Her tone suggested it was a perfectly reasonable activity. 'I'm afraid I'll have to take a few of the things you bought me as I no longer have any of my own clothes. But I'll reimburse you for them as soon as I find a job back in England.'

'Don't be ridiculous. I don't want you to pay for them.' He frowned as the meaning of her words sank in. 'You're not going anywhere.'

She still avoided looking at him, and in frustration he spun her round and slid his hand beneath her chin to force her to meet his gaze. The shimmer of tears in her eyes made his insides clench. 'You're upset.'

'Of course I'm upset that Sophie doesn't have a father.' She swallowed. 'You would have been a wonderful daddy to her. But now she'll grow up without a father, just as I did.'

Cesario's enigmatic expression gave away nothing of his thoughts, but Beth could guess what was going on behind his cool grey stare and she hated the idea that he was judging her.

'I know what you must be thinking,' she cried wildly. 'You think I brought Sophie to Sardinia to try and get money out of you. But I swear I only came because I believed Mel and I thought—if there was a chance that she was yours—Sophie deserved to know the identity of her father.'

'I know that.' His quiet statement stopped her in her tracks.

She stared at him uncertainly. 'You don't think I tried to con you because you're wealthy?'

'No.' There was no doubt in his mind. 'I've said before that I think you are utterly incapable of lying, *cara*.'

'But…in the nursery you looked angry.'

'I'm disappointed that Sophie isn't mine,' he admitted roughly. 'I'm not good at showing my feelings—it's not something I was ever encouraged to do.' He sighed. 'I think I understand the reason for the confusion. Did Mel actually show you the newspaper photo she said she'd recognised me from?'

Beth shook her head. 'No. When I visited her in hospital she was excited that she had discovered who Sophie's father was, but the cleaning staff had taken the paper away and I never saw it. But I believe Mel *did* see a photo,' she insisted.

'So do I—which is why I asked the PR department at Piras-Cossu to check the files for any articles about me or the bank that appeared in English newspapers in the first weeks of November last year. Sophie was born at the end of October, and you told me her mother died two weeks later, so Mel must have seen a photograph of the man she had slept with some time in those weeks.' Cesario handed

Beth a sheet of paper. 'My PR people just faxed me this. Only one article about Piras-Cossu appeared in the English press during that time—and I'm sure this is what Mel saw.'

Beth stared at the copy of the newspaper page. Below the title High Street Bank Profits Soar was a photo of a group of men in suits who were clearly bank executives.

'That's you, in the centre of the picture.' She frowned. 'But—if you didn't sleep with Mel why did she recognise you?'

'I don't think she did. I think she recognised someone else. Look at the list of names printed at the bottom of the photograph. They've been listed in the wrong order. The name beneath my picture is Richard Owen—who is actually the UK managing director of Piras-Cossu and is standing to the left of me.'

'And the name Cesario Piras is printed beneath the photo of the man on the right of you,' Beth said slowly. She snatched a breath, feeling as though she had been winded as she studied the image of a young, good-looking man standing beside Cesario. 'Anyone who looked at the photo would assume that this man was Cesario Piras. Did he attend the party in London a year ago? Could he be the man Mel spent the night with?'

'He was certainly at the party,' Cesario confirmed.

'But that means *he* must be Sophie's father. Mel didn't know his name, but she thought she had discovered his identity from the newspaper, unaware that the paper had made a mistake. Oh, God, I can't believe a stupid reporting error has caused so much confusion.' She sank onto the bed, feeling sick as the implications sank in. 'I'm so sorry. I should have made more checks before I brought Sophie here and accused you...'

She could not bear to look at Cesario. He had every

right to be furious with her, she acknowledged bleakly. What a fool she had been. But she'd had no reason not to take what Mel had told her as the truth. And Mel hadn't deliberately misled her—she'd made a mistake because of the misprint in the newspaper.

She tensed when Cesario sat down on the bed, but to her relief his voice held no anger. 'You're not to blame,' he said quietly. 'You were grieving for your best friend and trying to cope with a newborn baby. Mel had asked you to find her baby's father and you were determined to carry out her last wishes.'

Beth stared back at the photo. 'So who is this man who we think could be Sophie's father?'

'Luigi Santori—he was a junior executive at the bank and had been transferred to work at the London branch.' Cesario grimaced. 'He had a reputation for sleeping around, and it wouldn't surprise me if he'd had a one-night stand with Mel.'

Something in Cesario's tone made Beth dart him a puzzled look. 'Why do you speak about him working for the bank in the past tense? Where is he now?'

'He was killed in a motorbike accident three months ago.'

'Oh, no...' A chill ran through Beth. 'Then Sophie is an orphan.' For a moment she felt overwhelmed by the realisation that Sophie was entirely her responsibility. 'Poor little girl,' she whispered. 'At least I had my mother until I was twelve. Sophie will never know either of her parents, and I am the only person she has to take care of her.'

'That's not true.'

Cesario jerked to his feet and walked over to the window, his hands thrust into his trouser pockets and his shoulders rigid with tension. 'You could stay here—you and Sophie. And I could…'

To Beth's frustration he did not finish the sentence. She stared at his back, wishing he would turn around so that she could see his face and maybe understand what he meant.

'What could you do?' she said at last, when the silence between them had stretched her nerves to snapping point. 'I don't understand. Sophie is not your child—so I'll take her back to England and make a life for us.'

'What kind of life can you give her, struggling to get by as a single mother and trying to juggle holding down a job with bringing up a child?' Cesario demanded. He swung round. 'I care for Sophie.' It was so alien to him to express his feelings, but when Beth had said she planned to return to England it had struck him forcibly that he did not want to lose her *or* the baby girl who had filled the hole in his heart left by the loss of his son.

'I could pay—'

'No!' Beth cut him off instantly.

'For Sophie to have ballet lessons, holidays—all the things you wished for when you were a child and that you won't be able to afford to give her on your own.' He ignored her interruption. 'Is your pride more important than Sophie's welfare, Beth?'

'No, but…' She shook her head, trying to marshal her thoughts. 'You don't have to support me and Sophie. We are nothing to you.'

'You know that's not true. I have grown to love Sophie.'

Cesario felt like a blind man, trying to feel his way along a path he'd never travelled before. It was hard for him to expose his feelings, but at least talking about Sophie was easier than facing up to how he felt about Beth. He didn't *know* how he felt; he just knew that he had found something with her that he'd never had with any other woman—and he wasn't ready for their relationship to end.

'What I'm suggesting is that I become Sophie's joint guardian and that the two of you live here at the castle. I am a father without a child, and Sophie is a child without a father,' he said deeply. 'I want to be a part of her life.'

Beth stared at him, shaken by the strength of emotion in his voice. 'What about me? You can't mean you want me to stay here? But I will never leave Sophie. I intend to be a mother to her like I promised Mel.'

'Why shouldn't you stay here?'

Cesario strolled back over to the bed where Beth was still sitting. He no longer seemed tense, but beneath his indolent stance she sensed his formidable strength and a determined purpose that worried her almost as much as the glitter in his grey eyes. Her heart suddenly began to beat uncomfortably fast and she jumped up from the bed. She felt an urge to run from the room, from him, but before she could take a step he snaked his arm around her waist and pulled her against him.

'Why not stay?' he said again, his gaze locked with hers as if he could see into her soul. His voice dropped to a husky growl. 'The passion we share is beyond anything I have ever experienced before. We both felt an overwhelming awareness of each other on the night you arrived at the castle and even though we both fought it ultimately we could not deny our mutual desire.'

He lifted a hand and smoothed her hair back from her face. 'We have become friends as well as lovers these past weeks, haven't we, *cara*?' he murmured. 'We both love Sophie. Let me take care of both of you and help you to give her the happy childhood that we were both denied.'

A hundred questions hurtled around Beth's mind. How long did he want her and Sophie to stay at the Castello del Falco? Was he really offering the baby a home in Sardinia? What would his role in Sophie's life actually be—a father figure, a benevolent uncle? She gnawed on her lip, tormented by uncertainty. What role would he expect *her* to play in his life? They were lovers now, but what would happen in the future when he tired of her as he surely would?

She sensed he was waiting for her to answer, but she was finding it hard to think straight when she was desperately conscious of his big, muscular body pressed so close to hers that she could feel the hard ridge of his arousal nudging between her thighs.

'I don't know what to do,' she whispered.

Cesario cupped her face in his hands. She had such a beautiful face. Even when he closed his eyes her features were imprinted on his mind: her slanting green eyes, the sweep of her long eyelashes, the gentle curve of her smile. He felt a rush of tenderness that seriously undermined his determination to cling to the belief that the reason he wanted Beth to stay with him was because they had great sex.

'Do what your heart tells you,' he found himself saying. He—who always followed his head and never listened to his heart. He slanted his lips over hers and kissed her, slowly and sweetly, making him ache inside. She opened her mouth beneath his and he groaned and crushed her to him, sliding his hand to her nape and gently tugging her head back so that he could plunder her lips with heated passion. He was aware that his heart was telling him something, but he was afraid to listen. He told himself that it was just desire he felt for her—just a sexual hunger that had ensnared him and seemed unlikely to fade any time soon.

He hooked his fingers beneath the straps of her top and dragged them down until her breasts spilled into his hands. Tenderly, almost reverently, he caressed the small rounded globes, and then he lifted her up so that he could take first one taut nipple and then its twin into his mouth, suckling her until she gasped his name.

Beth gave up trying to fight her need for Cesario to make love to her. This was where she wanted to be, in his arms, with his hands feverishly stripping them both of their clothes. He tumbled her down onto the bed and she wrapped her arms around his neck, pulling him down onto her and loving the feel of his naked skin on hers, the roughness of his chest hairs against the softness of her breasts.

He slid his hand between her legs and found her already wet and eager for him. Her soft smile shattered any hope he had of a slow, leisurely loving, and he slanted his mouth over hers at the same moment as he eased the swollen length of his arousal into the welcoming heat of her femininity.

He took her fast and hard, and yet with such tender consideration that Beth felt tears sting her eyes as she reached that magical place and her body convulsed in the throes of an exquisite climax. Cesario came almost simultaneously, unable to control the wildfire pleasure that he always experienced with Beth.

Afterwards they lay together in a tangle of limbs while their breathing gradually returned to normal. He propped himself up on one elbow and smiled at the sight of her flushed cheeks and softly swollen mouth.

'So you'll stay.'

It was a statement rather than a question, as if there had never been any doubt. But as Beth watched him stand up from the bed and stroll into the *en-suite* bathroom the reality of the situation caused a host of doubts to gather like black clouds in her mind. They hadn't discussed the practicalities of her and Sophie living at the castle, but the more she thought about it the more pitfalls she could see.

'I'll need to find a job,' she said when he walked back into the bedroom five minutes later, rubbing his wet hair on a towel. 'I'm grateful for your offer to help support Sophie financially, but I'm responsible for her myself and I can't allow you to keep me for...' She hesitated. 'Well, for however long I'm here...' she finished uncertainly.

The idea of living on hand-outs from Cesario was abhorrent to her pride. She had grown up in the children's home, hating the feeling that she was reliant on charity, and since she'd left school she had always worked to support herself. She would have to take a crash course in Italian, she fretted, and then maybe she could find work in Oliena—although who would look after Sophie while she was working?

Cesario pulled on his trousers and took a clean shirt from the wardrobe before he walked over to the bed.

'We'll discuss things when I get back,' he murmured, leaning over her and brushing his lips across hers.

Maybe a few days away from her would clear his mind and help him to decide what he actually wanted, he thought. He knew he had surprised Beth when he'd asked her to stay with him. Hell, he'd surprised himself. It wasn't unreasonable of her to want to know if he had a timescale in mind, but, strangely, the more he thought about it the more insistently the words *for ever* pushed into his brain.

The sound of the helicopter landing in the courtyard was

almost a relief. He had four days of intense business nego-
tiations ahead and he needed to focus, concentrate—not
let his mind wander to a girl with green eyes and a smile
that turned his insides to jelly.

He kissed her mouth, lingeringly, and wondered briefly
if he could send one of his top executives to Japan in his
place. 'Four days isn't long.' He did not tell her it sounded
like a lifetime. He picked up his jacket and walked across
the room, but hesitated in the doorway and turned back
to her.

'Hurry back,' she said softly.

'I will...*tesoro*...'

And suddenly everything made sense to Cesario. He
stared at her, his heart pounding, but then his phone rang
and he knew it was his pilot reminding him he had to leave
now if he was going to make it to the airport in time to
catch his flight to Japan. This wasn't the moment to ask
Beth about for ever.

His eyes held hers. 'I didn't say it earlier, but you make
me happy too,' he said gruffly. 'I'll see you soon, *mia
bella*.'

The castle felt empty without Cesario—and so did Beth.
She kept reminding herself that he wouldn't have told her
she made him happy unless it was true, but in the long
sleepless hours of the night her doubts multiplied like
weeds after a rain shower. She did not doubt that he cared
about Sophie. And the way he had looked at her before
he had left for Japan made her think that perhaps he even
cared about her a little too. But could she really live as his
mistress, knowing that one day in the not too distant future he would tire of her?

He phoned once, but sounded distracted. He'd spent a

long day in the boardroom, he explained, and now he was
relaxing at his hotel. The woman's voice that Beth heard
in the background probably belonged to his PA, she told
herself. But the gremlin inside her head reminded her that
Cesario hadn't made any promises of commitment to her
and she had no right to ask him who he was relaxing with.

Cesario's affairs never last for long. Allegra Ricci had
told her that the night they had gone to the ballet. So how
long was long? Weeks? Months before his desire for her
died? Her old insecurities returned. She was the care home
kid who had always been overlooked by foster parents. No
one had wanted her then, and once Cesario's sexual interest in her faded she would become an encumbrance, tol-
erated only because he felt some misplaced sense of duty
towards Sophie.

Cesario felt a cramping sensation in his gut as the car
swept into the castle courtyard. Nervous tension was not
something he'd ever suffered from before and the experience was not pleasant. He was dog-tired, but that was
hardly surprising when he had worked eighteen-hour days
in order to push the Japanese deal through early. He ran
his hand over the stubble on his jaw and gave a rueful grimace. He needed a shower, a drink, and Beth—in reverse
order, he acknowledged as he felt the familiar tug of anticipation in his groin.

He wondered if she had missed him as much as he had
missed her. The car drew to a halt, and when his driver
opened the door he took a deep breath before he climbed
out. He recalled the unguarded expression in Beth's eyes
when she had asked him to hurry back, and he slipped
his hand into his pocket to curl his fingers around a small
square box.

Dio! Butterflies wearing clogs were dancing in his stomach. But he had never put his heart on the line before—and the prospect of what he was about to do was frankly terrifying.

He nodded to his driver and ran up the front steps. He was disappointed that it was Teodoro who walked across the hall to greet him, not Beth, but, *Madonna*, the mood he was in he was almost tempted to kiss the elderly butler, who had been more of a father figure to him than his own father had ever been.

It took a few seconds for him to realise something was wrong. Teodoro's usually inscrutable face was visibly upset.

'What is this?' he demanded as the butler handed him an envelope. 'Where's Beth?'

'She left the castle with the *bambina* yesterday.'

Cesario stared at his name written in Beth's neat handwriting. The butterflies in his stomach had gone, leaving behind a hollow nothingness. For a moment he was seven years old again, running into the castle to see his mother. Teodoro had handed him a letter then too—a brief note from her, telling him that she was sad she'd had to leave him but promising that she would always think of him. He didn't know if she had kept her promise because he had never seen her again.

He dragged his mind back to the present. There could be a number of reasons for Beth's unexpected departure, he told himself. But his hands shook as he ripped open the envelope and skimmed his eyes down the page.

The agency I used to work for phoned to offer me an interview for a job as nanny with a family on the south coast of England. It sounds ideal as they are

*happy for me to combine caring for Sophie with look-
ing after their two children. The position comes with
my own living accommodation, and it will be a wonderful place to bring up Sophie and allow me to be
independent. You have no responsibility for either of
us, and I could not live as your mistress indefinitely.*

Thirty years after reading the note from his mother,
Cesario once again experienced a gut-wrenching sense of
abandonment—but this time he could not burst into tears
and cling to Teodoro. *Big boys don't cry,* he reminded himself grimly, and Piras men never revealed their emotions.

Instead, he screwed Beth's letter up in his fist and
avoided the sympathetic expression in Teodoro's eyes as
he strode into his study and took a bottle of bourbon from
the drinks cabinet. Clearly, he had been wrong to think
Beth had feelings for him, to hope that she loved him. It
was lucky he hadn't revealed *his* feelings. Lucky he hadn't
made a fool of himself by telling her… He laughed bitterly and stared at the little square box on the coffee table
in front of him. He'd chosen emeralds to match her eyes,
and diamonds because, like her, they were pure and spar-
kling and utterly beautiful.

He leaned back and rested his head on the top of the
sofa. His throat ached. Maybe he was coming down with
a virus? His eyes felt gritty and he squeezed them shut,
ashamed of the hot wetness that seeped beneath his lashes.

Maybe there was something wrong with him—something that made him unlovable and drove the people he
cared about to leave him? His mother, his wife… He hadn't
loved Raffaella when he'd married her; they had both married for duty. But after their son had been born they had

grown closer, and the discovery that she was having an affair had hurt him—although he had never shown it.

He drained his glass, feeling the alcohol seep into his frozen blood. Raffaella and Nicolo were dead, and now Beth had gone, leaving him alone once more.

Something brushed against his leg and he opened his eyes to find Beth's scruffy dog sitting at his feet. 'Okay, not completely alone,' he acknowledged, reaching out to stroke Harry. The dog flopped down at his feet and howled mournfully. 'You and me both, mutt,' Cesario muttered, feeling the sound of the animal's grief slice through his heart. 'At least you know she cared about you.'

Every time Beth had fussed over the dog and said 'Love you, Harry,' Cesario had felt a stab of envy as he'd imagined her saying those words to him.

But why would she have done when he had never given her any real indication of how he felt about her? He poured himself another whisky, but instead of drinking it he swirled the amber liquid around the glass.

It wasn't surprising that Beth's unhappy childhood had made her wary and untrusting. Abandoned by her father, she had been devastated by the deaths of her mother and her best friend. Everyone she had ever loved had left her.

Yet she had given herself to him with absolute trust and told him she wanted him to be the first man to make love to her. He couldn't believe that had meant nothing to her. She had chosen to give her virginity to him, and every time they had made love these past weeks she had given herself so sweetly…so lovingly—as if she wanted to show him with her body what she did not have the courage to say in words.

So why had she left? He raked a hand through his hair. It didn't make sense. He must be wrong. Maybe he'd imagined that soft look in her eyes because he'd wanted to see it.

'*You make me happy,*' she'd once told him. Surely she wouldn't have said it unless she'd meant it? Beth was fiercely honest; it was one of the qualities he loved most about her—that and her gentle smile and her beautiful green eyes, the way she stroked his hair in those moments of sweet lethargy after they had made love.

Love! Cesario gave a hollow laugh. It was an emotion he had been denied during his childhood and it had been missing for most of his adult life. He had loved his son, but Nicolo's death had nearly destroyed him and he had vowed never to love anyone again when he knew how much pain it could bring.

He was in pain now; there was a terrible ache in his chest, a wrenching sensation of loss. But one thought drummed in his head. He had made Beth happy once and he was not going to let her go without trying to find out what had gone wrong. Determination replaced his despair and he jumped to his feet and strode to the door to call Teodoro.

'I need to fly to England tonight. See if you can book me onto a flight, and arrange for the helicopter to take me to the airport.'

The road that twisted up the mountainside was dappled gold from the setting sun, and the great jagged peaks all around were stained fiery orange. As the taxi turned a bend the Castello del Falco appeared, ancient and mellow in the fading light, its gates flung wide open as if they were welcoming Beth home.

The taxi drew up in the courtyard and the driver unloaded her bags while she lifted Sophie in her baby-carrier from the car. He was the same man who had driven her from the castle down to Oliena the previous day, and he was clearly intrigued.

'You will stay here for long?' he queried in broken English.

Beth gave him a tremulous smile. 'I hope so.' She did not add that if the master of the Castello del Falco refused to see her she would need the taxi driver's services again. There was a good chance that Cesario would not want to listen to her, but she had to try.

Waiting for her flight at the airport yesterday, she had finally faced up to why she had left him. She had been too scared to stay. The job opportunity had provided a good excuse for taking Sophie back to England. But the real reason she had run away was because she was afraid to accept the relationship Cesario had offered her, with all the uncertainty that being his mistress would mean.

Like a spoilt child, she had been disappointed that he hadn't offered what she had secretly hoped for. He hadn't acted like Prince Charming in the fairy tale and declared his undying love for her, then swept her off to a church to put a ring on her finger. But he was a man, not a fantasy character. A man, moreover, who had known pain and loss and who had been taught to hide his emotions.

Despite his past and his self-acknowledged difficulty in revealing his emotions Cesario had admitted that she made him happy. He had said he wanted a relationship with her, and just because he hadn't said it with hearts and flowers she had put her pride before her love for him and gone away to sulk.

She had never told him how she felt about him, Beth thought guiltily. Maybe he wouldn't want to hear her confess her feelings for him, and maybe he would tell her he did not want a mistress who was in love with him, but that was a risk she would have to take—because she wasn't ashamed of loving him and she was no longer prepared to hide her feelings.

Teodoro could not hide his surprise when he opened the front door and saw Beth. 'The master is at the stables,' he told her as she handed him the baby carrier in which Sophie was fast asleep. 'You should hurry to find him,' he called after her as she ran down the castle steps. 'He is due to leave for England this evening.'

The way to the stables was familiar to her now, but when she arrived Cesario wasn't there. Heart thumping, she continued up the mountain path—but stopped dead when a figure hove into view.

He was astride his great black horse, a dark silhouette against the setting sun. But as he approached his features became visible; his face was as hard as if it had been carved from granite, the scar running down his cheek half hidden by his long dark hair. From the proud set of his shoulders and the arrogant angle of his head he might have been a king from ancient times, powerful, inscrutable and as uncompromising as the mountains behind him.

He halted on the path a little way ahead of Beth, and even from a distance she could see the fierce tension that gripped him.

'You came back.'

The words sounded as though they had been torn from his soul. For a few moments he regarded her silently, before he dismounted and strode towards her.

Beth watched him—the master of the Castello del Falco, the only man she would ever love. She had planned to remain calm and discuss their relationship sensibly. But as

Cesario came closer and she saw the haunted expression in his eyes her composure cracked, and with an agonised cry she flew along the path and into his arms.

'*Dio*, if you ever leave me again...' Cesario's voice broke as he crushed her against his great chest and threaded his fingers in her hair.

His eyes blazed with an expression she was afraid to define. How had she ever thought them cold? she wondered. But then all her thoughts were obliterated when he claimed her mouth with savage possession and kissed her endlessly, passionately, and yet with such exquisite tenderness that tears slid down her face.

'*Tesoro...*' He tasted salt on her lips and his hands shook as he brushed away the trails of moisture from her cheeks. 'Why did you leave? I was about to fly to England tonight to find you.'

His words brought Beth crashing back to reality and she pulled away from him. It was time to be honest. But her voice faltered when she spoke.

'I got to the airport before I realised I couldn't run away,' she admitted.

'Why did you feel you needed to run from me?' Cesario demanded in a driven tone. 'You told me I made you happy, and we both know you are incapable of lying, *carissima*. Are you really interested in the job as a nanny, or is there another reason you want to go back? Tell me, is there some man in England you care about?' He voiced the jealous thought that burned like acid in his gut. 'If so, then why did you choose me to be your first lover?'

Beth's heart ached at the raw emotion in his voice. She stared at his scarred, beloved face and could not deny her feelings to herself or to him.

'There is no one else. And there never will be—because

I love you,' she told him fiercely, 'with all my heart. For the first time in my life I have felt special. I was always the care home kid—unimportant, unloved. But since I came to the Castello del Falco you've treated me with kindness and respect and trust. You made me feel beautiful and… and proud of who I am.' Her voice shook. 'For all those things, and more, I will love you for ever.'

Whatever else she might have said was lost beneath the pressure of Cesario's mouth on hers as he held her so close that she could feel the thunderous beat of his heart echoing in time with her own. He kissed her until she sank weakly against him, parting her lips beneath his and kissing him back with beguiling sweetness, so that Cesario did not know if it was her tears he could taste or his own.

'*Ti amo*, Beth. I love you with my heart and soul and everything I am,' he said roughly, his voice shaking with the force of emotions storming through him.

He felt as if a dam had held back his feelings for so many years, but now the dam had burst open, allowing the healing power of his love for the woman in his arms to sweep away all the pain that had gone before.

'You really love me?' she whispered, and the half-wondering, half-fearful expression in her eyes made his heart clench.

He knew what it was like to grow up without being loved, and he vowed that he would tell Beth every day how much she meant to him.

'Will you stay with me, *carissima*?' He paused for a heartbeat and then, to her startled surprise, dropped down onto one knee. 'Will you marry me, Beth Granger? I love you, and you love me, and we both love a little girl who needs us to be her parents.'

He felt in his shirt pocket for the little square box he

had been carrying next to his heart, and heard her startled gasp when he opened the lid and took out the teardrop emerald surrounded by diamonds that glittered in the golden rays of the sunset.

'With this ring, I promise to love you and cherish you for eternity,' he said softly as he slid the engagement ring onto her finger. 'I will repeat that vow in the chapel on the day you become my wife.' He looked into her eyes, his own blazing with his love for her. 'Will you, Beth?'

The faint note of uncertainty in his voice brought a lump to Beth's throat. Beneath the strong and powerful man she glimpsed the vulnerable boy who had been taught that love was a weakness. She knew how hard he found it to reveal his emotions, but she would make sure he knew every day that he was loved.

'I will,' she assured him.

And there was no need to say anything more as Cesario swept her up and carried her back to the castle, pausing on the steps to kiss his soon-to-be bride—much to the satisfaction of Teodoro, who hurried to inform the rest of the staff to prepare for a wedding.

* * * * *

A sneaky peek at next month...

MODERN™

INTERNATIONAL AFFAIRS, SEDUCTION & PASSION GUARANTEED

My wish list for next month's titles...

In stores from 18th May 2012:

☐ A Secret Disgrace – Penny Jordan

☐ The Forbidden Ferrara – Sarah Morgan

☐ Enemies at the Altar – Melanie Milburne

☐ In Defiance of Duty – Caitlin Crews

In stores from 1st June 2012:

☐ The Dark Side of Desire – Julia James

☐ The Truth Behind his Touch – Cathy Williams

☐ A World She Doesn't Belong To – Natasha Tate

☐ In the Italian's Sights – Helen Brooks

☐ Dare She Kiss & Tell? – Aimee Carson

Available at WHSmith, Tesco, Asda, Eason, Amazon and Apple

Just can't wait?

Visit us Online

You can buy our books online a month before they hit the shops! **www.millsandboon.co.uk**

0512/01

 **2 Free Books!**

 Get your free books now at
www.millsandboon.co.uk/freebookoffer

Or fill in the form below and post it back to us

THE MILLS & BOON® BOOK CLUB™—HERE'S HOW IT WORKS: Accepting your free books places you under no obligation to buy anything. You may keep the books and return the despatch note marked 'Cancel'. If we do not hear from you, about a month later we'll send you 4 brand-new stories from the Modern™ series priced at £3.49* each. There is no extra charge for post and packaging. You may cancel at any time, otherwise we will send you 4 stories a month which you may purchase or return to us—the choice is yours. *Terms and prices subject to change without notice. Offer valid in UK only. Applicants must be 18 or over. Offer expires 31st July 2012. **For full terms and conditions, please go to www.millsandboon.co.uk/freebookoffer**

Mrs/Miss/Ms/Mr (please circle)

First Name

Surname

Address

Postcode

E-mail

Send this completed page to: Mills & Boon Book Club, Free Book Offer, FREEPOST NAT 10298, Richmond, Surrey, TW9 1BR

Find out more at
www.millsandboon.co.uk/freebookoffer

Visit us Online

0112/P2XEA/REV